THE NOTORIOUS LORD SIN

TAMARA Gill

COPYRIGHT

The Notorious Lord Sin
The Wayward Woodvilles, Book 9
Copyright © 2022 by Tamara Gill
Cover Art by Wicked Smart Designs
Editor Grace Bradley Editing, LLC

ISBN: 978-0-6455467-8-1

PROLOGUE

London Season, 1809

Miss Paris Smith sat in the library of her best friend, the Duchess of Romney, and fought not to fidget. Today all her dreams would come true. The man who had captured her heart from the very first moment she had laid eyes on him just weeks ago was to call upon her. That he had asked to do so could only mean one thing.

She was about to become betrothed.

The thought made her stomach flutter, and she placed a hand there, fighting to remain calm. For several days now, her stomach had not been settled, and she could only hope the nerves would be gone forever after today. Replaced by happiness and love.

Knocking on the front door echoed through the house, and within a minute, she heard the muffled voice of the butler letting in Lord Astoridge.

She closed her eyes, drinking in the sound of him. His

deep baritone made her knees weak and caused delicious heat to pool where no heat ought to pool in an unmarried woman such as herself.

Now was the time.

Finally, he would ask her, and they would be together forever.

"Lord Astoridge is here to see you, Miss Smith," Thomas said, gesturing for the viscount to enter.

His lordship with his wide shoulders and tall, commanding presence towered over both her and the butler, and she smiled in welcome.

"Lord Astoridge, how good of you to call. Do sit down," she said, not wanting to appear too eager. Although, she was probably well past that. Her body flushed with need, giddy at the idea of him asking her to marry him, to be his wife and make good on his promise.

He nodded and sat on the settee across from her, his hands folded in his lap. She studied him and noted the light sheen of sweat on his brow.

Paris bit back a grin. She supposed when a gentleman was about to propose to a lady, it was common and expected that he would be a little nervous.

Especially if her answer was so very important to him, which she hoped it was. Just as consequential as his question was to her.

"Miss Smith, thank you for seeing me this afternoon. I hope you are well," he said, his attention on her fleeting before glancing back toward the unlit hearth.

Paris adjusted her seat to face him better and smiled, hoping that may ease his nerves. "I am well, thank you. I'm happy to see you," she admitted. Would this acknowledgment of her feelings help ask what he wanted? They had been courting for several weeks. He had danced with her multiple times, stolen kisses whenever the opportunity arose, and not to mention the one night at the Rossdale mask where a lot more than kissing passed between them.

All that they had shared only gave her certainty that he cared for her. That he wanted her as his wife, just as she so desperately wanted him to be her husband.

She sighed, studying him and all his handsomeness. His chiseled jaw, perfectly straight nose, and large, almond-shaped eyes, the deepest brown that, in a certain light, they appeared as dark as a moonless night.

"Miss Smith, it is only right that I call on you to be the gentleman I was brought up to be and offer you an explanation."

Paris schooled her features as dread settled in the pit of her stomach. "Explanation? Whatever do you mean, my lord?" How was a proposal an explanation pray?

He took a deep breath, closing his eyes a moment before meeting hers. "I've come here today, Miss Smith, to notify you and be honest in telling you that I cannot marry you." He paused and ran a hand over his jaw, watching her keenly. "The situation of my life and the ability to keep my estates, both here in England and France, means that I must marry a woman of substantial pars. Not to say that I'm in any way in a financial deficit. I am not, but the upkeep on my numerous estates means I must marry a woman who can support further those who live off my name and lands." He frowned, pausing. "I know you believed this visit this afternoon was for another purpose entirely, and I'm sorry to let you down in such a way. Know that should I not have so many people under my care, I would ask you to marry me. I would have picked you out of everyone else to be my wife."

3

Paris stared at his lordship, and for several minutes she could not form words of reply.

"Excuse me, my lord, but I must get this right. You're telling me you will not marry me because I have no dowry. That my lack of inheritance makes me invalid to be your wife even though, as you say, you're not in any way short of funds?" The room spun, and Paris clutched the sides of her chair to steady herself. "We were intimate, Dominic. I could be *enceinte*."

This could not be happening. The man she had pinned all her hopes on, whom she had thrown off other men for to be with, was now letting her down—telling her, in effect, that she was not good enough for him.

Not rich enough.

Poor little Miss Smith from Grafton, who reached too high within the cruel world of the *ton*. Who had given herself foolishly to a gentleman and now would pay the price of that folly.

He nodded and had the grace to look shameful. Paris swallowed the lump in her throat, sure if she did not, it would choke her.

"I apologize, Miss Smith if I allowed you to think there was more between us than there ever was. I did find you attractive, of course, you're a beautiful woman. You're amusing and kind, and we get along very well, but that is not enough for a man such as myself. I have responsibilities that must come first, even before my own wants and desires. I, therefore, cannot marry just because my heart tells me to. I must think with my head and what is best for my pocketbook."

Paris stood and paced before the unlit hearth, needing to do something before she would scream at the unfairness of what he was telling her. And while she had asked, she did not think he needed to be so honest and forthright in his reply.

"And do not worry about having a baby. A maid such as yourself is unable to fall pregnant during your first time. It has been medically proven, and if you do not tell your husband, whomever that may be, that you were intimate with me, he would not know," he answered so matter-of-factly that her heart crumbled in her chest.

"You have explained perfectly well why I'm not suitable, and I wish you well in finding your perfect match to your pocketbook, my lord," she said, not trying to hide the sarcasm in her tone.

"Miss Smith, please, do not be upset."

She raised her hand, stilling his words. "Upset? I think I have every right to be upset. You allowed me to believe that we were meant for each other for weeks. You made me care about you, and I trusted you. I'm sorry that you think I do not have the right to be *upset*. Maybe you ought to have thought of that before acting so sinful toward a woman you never intended to marry but merely tote along like some pathetic plaything that was an amusing trinket for the Season."

He stood, coming over to her. He tried to take her hands, and she yanked them away, stepping back. "Do not touch me, Lord Astoridge. You do not have the right."

He watched her, and she could see he was debating whether to listen to her command or attempt again to soothe her hurt feelings.

She ground her teeth, hoping for his own welfare that he did not try the latter.

"I never saw you as a plaything, Miss Smith. I'm sorry you feel that way," he answered, promptly halting any further explanation. "I think I should leave. I wish you all the very best with the remainder of your Season. Good afternoon," he said, bowing and striding from the room.

Paris watched him go, and with his leaving, all her hopes and dreams fled with him. Her stomach chose that moment to recoil, and she ran to the nearest potted plant and cast up her accounts.

CHAPTER
ONE

-

London, 1814

Dominic Parker, Viscount Astoridge, stood on the bow of an English frigate he had hitched a ride from France on and watched as London materialized out of the morning fog like a ghost of his past come back to haunt him.

He breathed deep the coal-thick, chill air of the city of his birth and wished he were back in France.

His mother's country estate, now his after the passing of his father, had made his years abroad a welcome reprieve, not that his pocketbook had fared very well.

After several failed investments, he was now in need of a rich wife, not merely to help finance his living but to ensure his younger twin sisters had the Season they deserved.

What a shameful homecoming to England.

Once anchored, it did not take him long to hire a hackney from the docks, and he was soon on his way toward his home on Mount Street.

How many years had it been since he had fled England? Three? Four? He leaned back in the squabs of the carriage that reeked of unmentionable scents and tried to remember.

"Five years." Thinking back to that dreadful day when he faced Miss Paris Smith and told her he would not offer marriage. What a cad and ass to be so unfeeling toward her. He had ruined her, taken her innocence, and had not looked back after he left London. Had never had the nerve to write his mother and ask what had happened to her. He hoped that she fared better than him, but a part of him knew that she possibly did not.

He ran a hand through his hair and sighed.

"Mount Street, the driver called as the carriage rocked to a halt. Dominic jumped down and threw up two silver coins before taking his valise and striding toward the front door.

His butler opened it before his foot hit the top step, and Dominic laughed. "Anyone would think you were expecting me, Malcolm," he said, handing his old retainer his traveling case.

"We were expecting you, my lord." He helped him with his greatcoat and hat. "There is a fire in the library, and I shall have Cook send in a light repast for you since it is past dinner and the ladies are out for the evening, my lord."

"Thank you," he said, entering a room he had relegated to his steward and one he had removed from his employment after finding out his business acumen was not what he professed it to be.

Not that Dominic could blame him entirely for his financial strife. He had lived a life of sin in France— gambling, entertaining, whoring, and making terrible decisions when under the influence, resulting in losing the majority of his inheritance.

He shook his head, walking to the tumbler of brandy and pouring a hefty glass. The burning, amber liquid did little to soothe his nerves. After a long day of travel or not, tonight he would have to start attending balls and parties. It was not much past nine, in any case.

He pulled the silver salver toward him, flipping through the invitations that had arrived.

One, in particular, stood out, and he pulled it out of the pile, reading it thoroughly. The Duke and Duchess of Romney were hosting their annual ball this evening.

He chewed his bottom lip, debating whether he ought to attend or not. Paris would be there if she were still in town since the duchess was her closest friend. That was if she had not fled back to Grafton and married a local boy from her town.

The idea made his eye twitch.

But no matter. He should not dwell on the past and what was lost to the pages of time. He needed to look forward to who would be his wife, and sooner rather than later since he did not know how to economize as well as he should have.

Later that evening, Dominic entered the Romney ballroom with Lord Lupton-Gage, his oldest friend since Eton. His wife, the marchioness, was home, preferring to stay with their small son and daughter for the evening.

"Thank you for coming with me, Gage. I admit that it has been many years since I stepped foot into an English ballroom. I'm very out of practice."

Gage laughed, tapping him on the back. "You will find your bearings, and there are many delightful young debutantes here this year who would make a suitable bride and future viscountess."

Dominic nodded and glanced about the room, noting the few interested coy gazes from several ladies. He nodded and smiled, as a gentleman would, but his heart wasn't in it. There was something off about what he was doing.

Even if he had voiced such a stance toward Miss Smith all those years ago of marrying an heiress, he had yet to follow through on his stipulation. He had instead traveled abroad and tried to increase his fortune before failing miserably at that as well.

Lord Lupton-Gage cleared his throat and glanced at him, an amused grin on his lips. "Prepare yourself, Astoridge. You're about to see a ghost."

Dominic frowned at his friend, and then he felt it, the prickling of the hairs on the back of his neck. He looked toward the doors, and time stood still.

No, that was not entirely true. It reversed, rushed back five years, and left him as besotted as the day he had first seen her across a ballroom floor.

Miss Paris Smith, the strawberry-blonde commoner from Grafton, was anything but what he had left, heartbroken and bereft in Romney's library five years before.

Oh no. The woman who walked into the room, bussing the cheeks of the Duchess of Romney, her laughter ringing out and capturing anyone who watched, himself included, was no shy mouse.

Not a timid miss who had coveted him only for him to break her heart. Who had trusted him with her innocence only for him to dismiss her as unworthy.

He could not tear his gaze from her as she made her way

through the throng of guests. She stopped before the Duke and Duchess of Derby and spoke to them, accepting a glass of wine from a passing footman.

For all her finery, the wealth that glowed from every diamond and silk stitch that she wore, she was still the same beneath it all. Her smile was as genuine, her speech engaging. No falsehood about her, not that there ever was.

What a fool he had been, not to mention an utter ass.

P aris reveled at being back in London. The past year of mourning had been hard for her, but mostly for her daughter and son, who missed their father terribly.

Lord Hervey had been a good man. He had loved her even though she knew at times she did not deserve his affection, but it was time that she returned to London to start to pave the way forward for her children when it was time for them to enter society.

She joined her close friend, Millie, now the Duchess of Romney, and settled beside her, more than happy for this evening to regain her bearings in society and see what everyone was about, but not take part too much.

"I'm so pleased you're here. How are Lady Maya and little Lord Hervey?" Millie asked her, always interested in her family and her happiness.

"All are thriving, and Oliver has assured me he will know all the kings and queens of England upon my return." She laughed at her son's fascination with all things royal and the history of this great land.

"How wonderful. I'm certain he will know all as promised." The duchess watched her a moment, and Paris frowned at the concern she read on her friend's face.

"What is it, Millie? You only look like you do when there

is something bothering you, and you're too scared to tell me."

Millie threw her a small smile, taking her hand in hers. "There is a certain person on tonight's guest list that I did not mention, for I did not think the guest would come to pass to attend, but he has."

A cold, hard knot settled in Paris' stomach, and she took a calming breath. No. It could not be, not after all this time.

She clamped her mouth closed and fought not to demand who Millie meant, raising the interest of everyone near them.

"You may invite whomever you please," she said, smiling to hide her discomfort. "There is no one here that can ruin my return to London and the Season. We shall have fun as usual unless it is Lady Smithers, and then I'll be dreadfully angry at you. You know how she dislikes that I married Lord Hervey, whom she had all but settled herself upon during our coming-out year together."

Millie chuckled, but Paris barely heard her friend's reply.

She clutched at her glass of champagne and fought not to faint as the room spun about her.

It could not be.

He would not dare.

She clamped her mouth shut, staring across the ballroom floor, unable to comprehend what her eyes were seeing.

Bile rose in her throat, and she swallowed hard. How dare he show his face here? How dare he look at her after how he had played her wrong? Used her and gave her hope when she was never good enough for him and his lofty family.

"Lord Astoridge is here, Paris," Millie whispered. "I'm sorry."

Paris took a calming breath and glared at his lordship, who continued to watch her as if he expected some gift of a smile, a small wave, or some friendly gesture that would make all his awful, treacherous doings go away.

They would not.

She would never forgive him for his ungentlemanly act. No matter how many years passed, her heart still stung at the thought of that day.

She had been so full of hope, all but ready to order the carriage and travel down to her modiste and have her wedding gown fitted.

He was a waste of her emotions and time, just as he was a waste of effort even now.

His lips lifted into a small smile, and she narrowed her eyes.

Do not come my way, Lord Astoridge. You are not welcome here.

He mentioned something to Lord Lupton-Gage at his side and started toward her. Paris swore, steeling herself to speak to him again. For five years, her devastation and ire had bubbled away. Each time she looked at her daughter, she was reminded of everything she had lost. If he were hoping for a sweet reunion, he would be mistaken. She was unlikely to make that error a second time.

CHAPTER
TWO

Dominic bowed before Paris and smiled, drinking in the sight of her after all the years he could not. She had barely changed and was as beautiful as he remembered her. A multitude of questions bounded about in his mind, and he needed to know all she had done. What path her life had traveled. From the look of her low-bodice, empire-cut gown of the finest silk, she had fared better than he.

"Good evening, Miss Smith." He stared at her, gathering his wits, sure they had fled him for a moment. The closer he was to her, the more he realized how very beautiful she had become.

More so than when he had first met her. He shook his head at the thought. She had turned into a woman in the five years since he had seen her last. A delicious, beautiful, worldly woman and the pit of his stomach clenched. "I'm so very happy to see you again," he admitted, the words as true as him standing before her.

"Lord Astoridge," she said, her words dripping with indifference. "I married the Earl of Hervey some years past.

I'm the Countess of Hervey now, Lady Hervey to you," she corrected him, her eyes as cold as her words.

Dominic's stomach churned at the knowledge she had married. How had he not known? When he had traveled to France, he knew his mother would not have notified him. She never cared for Miss Smith, but for his friends not to inform him, well, he could not help but wonder why.

He glanced about the room, searching for Lord Hervey. "I hope to congratulate your husband and yourself on your nuptials. They are long overdue."

She raised her brow, staring down at him with annoyance. "You will have to contend with only offering me your congratulations, my lord. Lord Hervey sadly passed away early last year," she explained, sipping her wine and watching him over the rim of her glass.

Dominic ignored the shocking realization that ran through his mind at that moment. Paris was unmarried. A widow. He frowned and fought to compose appropriate words that sounded heartfelt.

They would not be.

He had never liked Lord Hervey, not when he had tried to court Paris while Dominic was making his own interest known. He could go to hell for thinking in such a way, being near her again, smelling the sweet scent of lilies that always accompanied her, and falling under the spell of her beauty. He did not care to think ill of the dead.

"I'm very sorry for your loss, my lady," he lied. "I did not know."

"No, well, how could you? You were in Paris or somewhere abroad, I understand. We did not communicate, and I rarely came to Town these past two years due to my husband's health," she said, raising her brow as if she found his presence a bore. "Close friends and family were informed, of course, but no one else."

He ignored her barb and her aloofness toward him. Hell, he hoped she did not find him such a bore, a pain in her side that she could not remove. There had been a time when she had all but glowed at the sight of him. Such a long time ago now, but surely she was not still mad at him.

"Did you ever marry, my lord?" she asked him.

He glanced about the room. Several people watched them keenly. It was no secret that during the 1809 Season, he had courted Paris. Nothing ever came of it due to the familial duties that stopped him from marrying a woman of no fortune or influence. Harsh words he had long regretted, but they were done, and he could not take them back, no matter how much he wished he could.

He had broken her heart that afternoon, and from the cool reception he was receiving, Paris had not forgiven him.

Yet ...

"I did not, my lady. I traveled to France to oversee the running of my mother's French estate. It was in a dreadful state and needed much work," he explained. Not to mention he had made multiple mistakes that ensured he returned home and would all but beg for a rich bride before too long. "But I'm back in London now, and the Season is young. One never knows who shall cross one's path, and romance may ensue."

She scoffed, her lips twitching. "So you returned to find a rich wife. How ironic, my lord. I would not have expected that from you," she sneered.

"Our social spheres are of the highest echelon of society, my lady. It is often hard to find one who does not have some modicum of fortune when one falls in love," he said, rolling his shoulders to ease the tension that thrummed there. He was so full of cow dung. How could he say such things when they were untrue? Miss Smith had circulated in his sphere, and she had nothing, and he still wanted her.

This evening and his reunion with her were not going as planned.

"Is that so." She came and stood beside him, nodding in the direction of each lady whom she spoke of. "Miss Wilson is an only child and her father's property, the Honorable Baron Wilson is not endowed, so you would inherit a tidy sum and a hefty piece of land in pretty Somerset if you courted her." She paused, pursing her lips as she studied the ladies milling about before them. "Oh, Lady Esme Smithers, you already know is an heiress, fifty thousand pounds if the rumors are still true. I should think that would fill your coffers very well and please that familial duty of which you speak. Not to mention, Lady Esme is still vexed you courted me over her."

"Are you finished, my lady?" he asked, pinning her with a hardened stare. "You are being unkind."

She chuckled, sipping her wine. "Lord Astoridge, you ridiculous man. I'm not the least finished with you. I've only just begun," she said, her tone mocking.

"I do not need a lady's inheritance," he spat, her taunting getting the better of him. He nearly choked with the words from his lying tongue. He needed the blunt more than ever. He may be titled, but with two sisters about to join the Season now that he was in Town, and with debts to pay from his unfortunate investments, lean times were ahead unless he found an heiress, and soon.

But whom?

And how to get one without them knowing he needed their money much more than their loving heart.

Worse still, how would he keep such a secret from the

woman at his side? The one lady who knew when he spoke the truth. Or when he was hiding something.

An impossible task he could not fail at.

Paris delighted in getting under Lord Astoridge's skin. The man was a menace. Coming all the way back from Paris merely to enjoy the Season. A rich man and his folly in finding a suitable bride to satisfy his family's expensive taste that even his lordship had seemed to inherit.

"Of all things to say to me, do not lie again," she bit back. "And you never know, the ladies you court may wish to marry only for a title and a lovely country house. Just because you're not looking for a rich bride does not mean a lady is not looking for a rich husband." She chuckled, glancing at him before dropping her eyes. "Could you imagine that? You marry a woman for her money, and she, in turn, does the same to you. There is a sense of poetic justice in that, I think."

"I do not think ..."

"And fitting," she whispered to her shame. But the man vexed her dearly, and still, after these years, she could not forgive him. She had been forced to marry a man she did not love. A man she had grown to care for certainly, but nothing more than that. A man she shared a bed with, was intimate with, yet imagined another beside her all along.

For so long, she had yearned for Astoridge, and now, with him here beside her again, all she wanted to do was hurt him. Speak down to him. Ridicule him. Make him feel and hear all the horrible, unbearable, not-good-enough ways he had so lovingly bestowed on her.

Paris looked up, wanting to give him another set down, only to find him watching her. She inwardly swore. The man was still so annoyingly good-looking that it ought to be outlawed.

"That is unfair, my lady." He lowered his voice, stepping closer.

Paris ought to step back, not allow him to crowd her so, but the scent of sandalwood and something that was entirely Astoridge halted her steps.

She breathed in deep, to her chagrin, and fought to remain aloof.

"It's been five years, Paris. Why are you still disgruntled with me? You married an earl. One would think that you would be happy. You are a countess, after all."

But she had wanted to be a viscountess, she wanted to shout at him. A lower or higher rank she did not care for either. All that had mattered to her during her first Season was falling in love. Marrying a man who would make her as happy as her best friend had become marrying the Duke of Romney.

Not to mention all the other Woodville sisters who married men who loved them.

But of course, they had something Paris did not.

Money.

And Lord Astoridge deemed it appropriate to marry women who had plenty of it, even though he did not need funds. All to ensure the Astoridge's remained prosperous and rich.

How she wished to scold him more over allowing such a travesty to happen to their lives. To the genuine affection that had been between them.

"Disgruntled is probably not the correct term for how I feel about you now, my lord. I must admit that I no longer feel anything for you," she lied, knowing the declaration was false. Damn him to Hades. Still, after all these years, her body fought against her mind, savored the sight of him again, of remembering their one sinful evening. "In fact," she continued. "The moment I saw you at the ball, I had an overwhelming desire to have you removed. But," she sighed, speaking in half-truths, "this ball is hosted by my favorite friend, the Duchess of Romney, and I feel I owe her my best behavior. I think I have managed to be courteous quite well so far."

He nodded, clearing his throat. "We were friends once before we muddled up that connection with talk of marriage. Can we not be again? I never wished for our ease of speech, our ability to laugh and enjoy each other's company to end. You must know this."

She downed her wine and finished it. "Friends, my lord? I think the time for such companionship is at an end. And if you cannot remember when any affection I had for you vanished, I'll remind you." She tapped her chin, thinking of the worst day of her life. "That we were intimate before you so bluntly told me that I was not worthy of your hand but days later. In the Romney library, this very house if you need reminding," she said, watching him and enjoying the blush that stole across his cheeks. "But I do wish you well in wife-hunting. Do keep my suggestions in mind. You will not find better," she said, walking away, unable to hide the smirk from her lips.

CHAPTER
THREE

Dominic watched as Lady Hervey lifted her nose and strolled away without a backward glance. He soon lost her in the sea of heads and inwardly swore.

"Well, that did not seem to go as planned," Gage said at his side, cringing before handing him a glass of wine.

"No, it did not," he agreed. "She is angry with me, which is understandable, I suppose, but I thought after five years, we may be civil to one another."

Gage nodded sympathetically but looked less than convinced. "It may take time. She has not seen you in so long, and she has only recently come out of mourning. With the death of the earl, she has not been in town for over a year, and some of her decorum may be a little ... unpracticed."

"Unpracticed?" Dominic repeated. "I do not think that is the case. She knew what her words meant and how to strike at me. She's mad still, and there is little I can do about it."

Gage clapped him on the shoulder, gesturing to all the guests before them. "Mingle, dance, there is certain to be a young lady who suits you here, or at many other entertainments you shall attend in the coming weeks. Unless you're looking to make the widow Hervey your new viscountess?" Gage asked, pinning him with a stare.

Dominic's gut clenched at the thought. He liked the idea of Paris being his wife, even after all the years they were apart. She was once all he had ever wanted until his mother reminded him he had two sisters to marry and care for, and a good marriage for himself was paramount in throwing them into other suitable matches.

Not that he had to concern himself too much, for his sisters were only now coming of age. He could have married Miss Smith and secured her position in society for five years already, therefore not impacting his name in any way. Maybe her accounting may have been better than his, and he would not have found himself in such dire financial circumstances.

Miss Smith is penniless with no family connections worth a penny.

His mother's warning echoed in his mind as he caught a glimpse of Paris through the throng of guests. She spoke with Lord Spencer. The marquess was the same age as himself, and as rich as Croesus.

Unlike himself.

A penniless viscount.

He downed his wine, shame washing through him. He was a failure in every way. If society found out about his downfall, there would be no saving himself or his family's standing.

And he could not fail. His sisters needed to marry, and he was determined they all married well.

A hypocritical thing to do since he had not afforded the same courtesy to Miss Smith.

"She would not have me now, even if I wished to reconcile. I broke her heart, and she will not allow me to heal it, I fear," he admitted.

"Then I suggest you start to court a woman who appeals to you." Gage paused. "You are allowed to make mistakes in the past and be forgiven for them. I'm certain in time Lady Hervey will become a friendly acquaintance once more."

Dominic nodded but wasn't as sure. Paris seemed very cutting and angry still. Not to mention she did not need to remarry, not if she did not wish.

"Did she have any children with the earl?" he asked, drinking her in as she spoke freely with Lord Spencer.

Gage cleared his throat. "Yes, two. A daughter in their first year of marriage and then two years later a son."

Dominic ground his teeth as jealousy coursed through his blood. Two children and one an heir to keep the family line going. Two children he could have had with her had he been strong enough to refute his mother's demands. He had been so young then, new to being out in society and with a title. In truth, he did not know what he had been doing.

And now he was going to court a woman, become a scroff, a leech who married for money. Nothing but his good name keeping him and his family afloat in society.

Not that there were no families willing to marry penniless, titled gentlemen in exchange for their daughters stepping into the world of nobility and gaining a title.

But how could he face Paris if he were to marry under such circumstances? And the truth would come to pass. Society would become aware eventually of his impoverished state, and then she would hate him even more.

For he had become what he condemned her for. What he had stated so unemotionally was why he could not marry her.

What a bastard he was for treating what they felt for each other with so little respect. He would not blame her if she never spoke to him again.

He deserved no less.

P aris returned to the Duke and Duchess of Romney's side and breathed a relieved breath that she had survived her first meeting with a ghost of her past whom she had never wanted to encounter again.

Lord Astoridge being back in London meant one thing —that he was going to look for a wife and marry. After all the years he had lived abroad, she had been surprised that word of his marriage to some heiress and well-connected family had not reached her ears.

Seemingly he had not married at all.

But why?

When he had shunned her and broken her heart, why had he not set out and completed what his family so obviously wanted him to? But then, this year Lord Astoridge's sisters were to debut, and so maybe that was why he had returned to England. A good marriage for his lordship would assist his siblings in making a grand match.

Not that they would not. Each of them an heiress with money and a titled brother. There was little they coveted.

"How did your discussion go with Lord Astoridge? I saw you talking with him. You seemed to be conferring a great many things," the Duchess of Romney asked her.

"We spoke, but it wasn't as successful as I think he

would have hoped. If I'm brutally honest, I was less than pleasant, which is no more than he deserves."

Millie raised her brows, her eyes wide. "Well, that is true, but surely you do not still harbor ill will toward him. It has been five years, and you did marry a man you respected," Millie reminded her.

All true, of course, but to her shame, she had not loved Lord Hervey. He had been a reactional marriage to the heartbreak that she had suffered from Astoridge's denial. A marriage brought on by the near panic that she had missed her courses and was sick most mornings.

Not that Lord Hervey had ever been aware, and by the grace of God, she had birthed a daughter. If she had borne a boy, she wasn't so certain she could allow him to believe his heir was of his blood. Even now, the thought made her stomach churn.

With his lordship's pleasure at marrying her, she grew to like him very much, a friendship that was strong and true. But love? No, she never loved him. Not like she had once loved Lord Astoridge.

With merely the thought of him, her body was not her own. A woman now—more astute with the ways of marriage and what is possible between a man and woman —she knew what that emotion was when it came to the man she had loved and lost.

Desire.

She had desired Astoridge, had burned for him, and yet even if she had not known what those feelings meant at the time, she now did.

Lord Hervey had loved her well, and she had enjoyed their intimate times together.

But to think what she could have had with Astoridge,

knowing that adoration and passion, that kaleidoscope of feelings that would bombard her, made her skin prickle in awareness even now.

It would be an explosion of emotion.

"Lord Hervey, God rest his soul, was a good man and a wonderful father, and I shall always miss him. And I'm more than content to live out my days as a widow raising my young earl to take over his father's role and my daughter into a lovely young woman. Lord Astoridge need not waste his time with me, as I'm not looking for another husband."

"I'm sure he wasn't about to propose, Paris. He merely wanted to renew your friendship, I'm sure," Millie suggested, grinning.

Paris shrugged, wanting to ensure no one misunderstood anything. "Even so, I think it is best that no misunderstandings occur from the first reunion, such as the one we just had. I do not want him to think there is a possibility of us when there is not. I'm not certain I even like the man. There is much to think upon."

Millie nodded. "I think you have always harbored regret in what happened between you, and I will not allow you to lie to yourself or me. His being here could be a fortunate thing, Paris. You could marry him. You're rich enough now to be suitable."

And that was the rub. She did not want to be married merely because she now had money or because being so made her suitable. His equal. Lord Hervey did not marry her because of such a fickle and worthless status. He married her because he wanted to, because he cared for her, and loved her.

Lord Astoridge only loved his pocketbook.

"But is he rich enough for me? I do not think his morals are at the standard that I require to marry him. He broke my heart because I had no dowry. I'll not marry him because I now do so."

"Paris," Millie said consolingly. "I did not mean to offend. I just mean these men of influence and from grand families with titles dating back hundreds of years are brought up to think only of the family and what is best for them, how to keep the home fires burning, if you will. You must acknowledge that you are now thinking of such things with young Lord Hervey. You plan and prepare for when he comes of age so his estate is in the best shape it can be. Lord Astoridge would have been brought up the same. To marry women such as us, women from families that have very distant or no gentry relations is a gamble. You know you will think the same when it is time for Lord Hervey to marry. You will vet his bride and ensure she is suitable for him. I'm not certain we can judge Lord Astoridge too harshly for doing the same. He does have two sisters to care for."

Disappointment and annoyance thrummed through her at her friend's words. "Whose side are you on, Millie? He did not have to court me. He did not have to make me believe that I stood a chance at winning his heart, which need I remind you he did." She shook her head, biting her lip to stop the tears that always filled her eyes at the reminder of that horrible day in the Romney library. "He acted as though I was his sun and air, and then overnight, I was nothing but a passing folly. I will not forgive him, nor will I allow my son to treat any woman with such disrespect, and I hope you will not either," she said, turning on her heel and leaving. She could not listen to another word of Lord Astoridge and his poor choices that were not his own.

They *were* his own, and now he had to face the repercussions of that decision, even if it was seeing her at every event and party and witnessing all that he lost and would not get back again.

CHAPTER
FOUR

The following evening Dominic traveled to the Theatre Royal to attend an opera. It had been years since anyone had used the family box, his mother preferring to remain in the country when he was living in Paris and not attending the Season.

However, she was here this evening, having traveled up from Surrey to debut his sisters and enjoy the 1814 Season.

He entered the box, and his mother and two sisters greeted him with warm hugs and bussing kisses on his cheeks.

"My darling boy, I'm so happy to see you. I missed you at dinner, but Malcolm said that you were attending the opera after visiting your club, and I'm pleased that we are here together," she said, watching him for a moment before she went and took her seat.

"Good evening, Dom," his younger sister, but the elder of the twins, said, a mischievous light to her eyes before she, too, bussed his cheeks. "I hope this opera is not as boring as our curtsy to the queen was this afternoon."

"Oh, do be quiet, Anwen," Kate said with a sigh, curt-

29

sying before him as if he were a king. He rolled his eyes, wondering how he had gained two very determined and yet, at times, silly sisters. "You know as well as I that everything we are made to do during the Season shall be a bore."

Dominic chuckled, gesturing for his sisters to take their seats. "Please sit down and try to behave yourselves this evening. You must make a good impression if you're to marry well," he suggested. Needing them to make good matches, if only so they were not left old maids from lack of dowries.

Their box on the side of the theater offered a generous view of the stage and the other surrounding boxes that the *ton* occupied. He looked at each of his siblings and mama, wishing he could share the burden that shadowed his every thought.

If he could only marry a woman with a handsome dowry, his family would never have to sell such privileges as the box they now sat in or the fine clothes they wore.

The Astoridge family had held a box at the Theatre Royal for several decades. It would be a monstrous scandal if they were forced to let it go.

"I'm so looking forward to tomorrow for your sister's debut. Of course, it would have been a boon had you been settled by now so that your new wife would be willing to help present them. What fun we all shall have this year. All together again," she said, reaching over and clasping his hand. "We have missed you while you were away in France."

He met her gaze, seeing she was earnest in her words. "Are you not interested in how your ancestral home in France is faring?" he asked her. It was her childhood home, too, until she married the late Viscount Astoridge and relocated to England permanently.

His mama opened her fan and fluttered it before her. "I should imagine it is just as I left it. I do not know why you were so determined to live there for all that time. But I suppose there are just as many French heiresses as there are English ones, and I do only want the best for my son," she said, reminding him yet again that she was determined he marry a woman of means.

"All in good time, Mama," he said, hoping that was the end of that particular conversation.

His mother had been adamant that he disentangle himself from Miss Smith. Send her back to the country village of Grafton she came from. Not so easy to do when he had lain with Paris. Shame washed over him that he had stooped so low as to take her innocence and then cast her aside like waste.

His mother took in the other boxes, smiling and nodding in acknowledgment of those she knew. He watched her, knowing her attention would soon fall on the Countess of Hervey's box, and he was curious to see if Paris received any courtesy from his parent.

"I see Lady Hervey is here this evening. It has been barely a year since her husband passed, and she is already back in London looking for another. I hope you do not think to renew old acquaintances. We can do better than a woman from nobody knows where," his mother said, her bitter words losing none of their chill.

Dominic fought not to roll his eyes. His mother ought to be grateful for anyone who would seek his hand. If she only knew his predicament, she would not be so particular.

"Lady Hervey's mourning period is over, and she is more than welcome back into society as is her right. You cannot still harbor hostility toward her ladyship. She's no longer a country miss with no dowry, Mama. She is a rich and young titled widow and has a son to ensure the Hervey Earldom. Paris is very well situated," he mentioned, looking across to Paris's box and watching her as she laughed and spoke with the Duke and Duchess of Romney.

She was the very picture of elegance and beauty this evening. Her empire-style gown of shimmering green silk made her eyes sparkle, and her strawberry-colored hair stood out against all the others set to enjoy the opera.

"No eldest son of the Viscountcy Astoridge line has married a woman of nobody in the several hundred years of holding our title. Miss Smith may dress up as a countess, but she is as common as my modiste. Please do not speak of her again. It only upsets your mama," she said.

Dominic stopped listening to his mother's rambling. He would marry whomever he wanted and would not be persuaded otherwise ever again. Even if he wanted to marry someone other than Paris, he would do so and be damned what his mother thought. The time for being particular was over and had been so from when he lost all their money.

How could he have been such a fool?

He had fled London the moment he had injured Paris's heart, knowing that if he had stayed, he would have crumbled and begged her for forgiveness. He had drunk himself into oblivion and thrown himself into a life of ignorance instead. Took risks he would otherwise not have.

Not that he blamed Paris for the mishandling of his funds or his lifestyle. None of this was her fault. He was a cad, the murderer of hearts and feelings.

If only he could take it all back, he would.

But now, to save his family and ensure the survival of all his tenants and staff, he had to marry well.

Except even now, everyone else paled in comparison to Paris.

She looked across the theater, and their eyes met, held. The pit of his stomach clenched, and his heart stopped. Those striking eyes, her lips, and the swell of her breasts made longing rip through him. He wanted her still, and that was the rub.

How would he win her heart when she was determined to deny him? How could he convince her his affections were sincere and not motivated by his financial strife?

An impossible task perhaps, but one he was willing to undergo, even if the cost was his pride or his mother's sanity.

P aris watched as Dominic's attention was diverted from her when a young woman she had not seen before leaned over and spoke to him. There were two women present she had not seen before, sitting in the box with the viscount. Were they his sisters in town for the Season?

His mama, a woman who had never hidden her distaste for Paris, turned and greeted Lady Esme Smithers, who also seemed to be joining his lordship for the opera. Dominic's surprise at her attendance was telling, and she chuckled to herself, knowing only too well what the Dowager Viscountess Astoridge was up to.

Poor Lady Smithers seemed doomed to attempt to court men who had wooed Paris. Was the woman trying to get one up on her by making her interest known to Dominic?

Not that she would not be perfect for the viscount, considering she was an heiress and her father owned half of Kent.

The thought left a sour taste in her mouth.

"Lord Astoridge is here with his sisters and Lady Esme. Can only mean one thing," Millie said, raising her brows and turning to watch his lordship.

"And what is that?" Paris queried, not wanting to discuss his lordship at all. Not really. To do so only made her feel wretched and remember how he so cruelly used her and broke her heart.

"That he's searching for a wife." Millie met her eye, and Paris knew what her friend believed. That she ought to step forward and try to win his heart again.

She would not. The man deserved no forgiveness for something unforgivable. He had led her on a merry dance five years ago, and she had not forgiven him. Nor would she ever.

"Well, it seems that Lady Esme is certainly letting him know, if her delicate chuckles and fluttering eyelashes are anything to go by, that she's willing to be the next Viscountess Astoridge."

"You cannot possibly see her fluttering her eyelashes, Paris," Millie stated, laughing at her words. "We are too far away."

Paris shrugged but continued to watch the Astoridge box and the goings on within it. "Well, one can assume."

Lady Esme sat beside Lord Astoridge as his sister moved to sit elsewhere in the box. "His sisters are very handsome," Paris managed, narrowing her eyes at him. The simmering anger, mixed with the hurt that was always present, bubbled within her.

As if sensing her, he looked across the room. Their eyes met, held for a second time. The determination, the hunger in his dark eyes conjured a need within herself she had long denied.

Paris fought against the gnawing in her stomach, refusing to allow herself to feel anything for the man but contempt. As handsome as he was in his superfine coat, his broad shoulders and a face that would make weaker men weep, she would not fall at his feet a second time.

"He certainly is watching you a great deal, Paris. Even with the diversion of Lady Esme beside him. He is not looking at her for all her chattering and trying to gain his attention."

The theater staff snuffed the candles, and she turned her attention to the opera and took a deep, fortifying breath. She would not look at him again. Not this evening or ever if she could manage it. He may watch her all he liked. "It does not matter to me. I do not need his name or his money. I'm a countess, and he can go to the devil for all I care."

CHAPTER
FIVE

Dominic was determined to speak to Paris this evening. Even if she continued to ignore his presence and watch the opera without a flicker of awareness of what was going on about her.

Was she doing such a thing on purpose to him? Punishing him by pretending that he did not exist?

The inane chatter from Lady Esme beside him whenever she could get a word in between his mother and his sisters grew tiresome, and his mind wandered.

He looked back to where Paris and the duchess sat and noted during the opera's intermission their box was full of visiting friends, some siblings of the duchess, all of whom were from the same town of Grafton.

Regret sliced through him that he was not part of that world. Not really. He had been away for so long, and although Lupton-Gage was a close friend, he was the only one.

His choice five years ago ensured they rallied about Paris, and he was happy she had the support after he denied her marriage, but that did not change what he wanted now.

Paris...

"Lady Hervey is a beautiful woman, is she not?" Lady Esme said, pulling his attention back from her. He cleared his throat, having not expected such a compliment from her. Paris had often spoken of Lady Esme's dislike of her during their coming out, and he couldn't help but wonder what mischief she was leading to.

"There are many beautiful women at the opera tonight, yourself included," he added, wanting to compliment the young woman beside him. For all her beauty and wealth, he felt very little for the chit. Mayhap it was what he knew of her from Paris, or simply because he wanted someone else.

The woman he had thrown to the curb and had regretted his decision ever since.

"I understand she's recently back in town after the death of her husband, the earl. While I do not remember much of Lord Hervey," Lady Esme continued, "I heard they were a love match and very happy. I feel for Lady Hervey. I'm certain she misses him very much."

Dominic almost choked on his wine. He glanced at Lady Esme to see if she were in earnest in what she said and there was not even a smidge of blush on her cheeks at her blatant lie. The woman knew and had coveted Lord Hervey. Did not remember him, indeed.

But then she made a good point. Did Paris love and miss her husband? Had it turned into a love match? The thought made bile rise in his throat, and he swallowed hard.

How could he have let her go?

How the hell would he get her back when she wanted nothing to do with him? He was all but ruined financially.

He shook his head, at a loss of what he could do without looking like a scroff.

"If you will forgive me. I better make the rounds since I, too, have been away from London for some time," he said, excusing himself.

To ensure he did not appear too keen toward Paris, he visited several boxes on his way to where she sat for the evening. The conversation with those he visited first was benign and of little consequence, as much of what he spoke of was these days. The same chatter within the *ton* was often self-congratulatory and boring at best.

In time he made it to the duchess and countess's box, and thankfully, it had cleared out a little, allowing him to speak with her.

"Good evening, Your Grace, Lady Hervey," he said, bowing to them both.

The duchess smiled up at him. "Welcome, Lord Astoridge. It has been some years since I saw you last. How are you enjoying the Season?" she asked him, always polite and welcoming.

"Very well, thank you," he said, moving over to where Paris sat. She watched with an unnerving stillness that made his stomach clench. "Lady Hervey, I hope you're enjoying the opera?" he asked her, taking a seat at her side.

She sipped her wine, her eyes narrowing on him. "Why are you here, Lord Astoridge? You cannot still think that we can be friends after everything that has come to pass between us?" she whispered for only him to hear.

He turned to face her fully, hating that she disliked him so much. That he was so distasteful to her. Not that he did not deserve her ire. "I'm sorry, Paris. I do not know what else to say to you other than I'm so deeply sorry for hurting you, but can we not be friends again? We used to share all confidences. I want that again with you," he admitted.

She chuckled, but the sound held no amusement. "Friends?" She leaned toward him, her breasts pushing up against her silk bodice, and he fought not to look at her luscious curves. "We were never friends. You knew I loved you, thought you loved me, which you allowed me to believe, and yet so cruelly and without feeling, you rejected me due to being common. I do not think there is a way forward from here." She gestured toward his box, a knowing smile on her kissable lips. "Lady Esme is more suitable for you. She is an heiress, just what you're after, is she not? Must keep Mama happy." Her barb hit him in the middle of his chest.

"What if I do not want anything from you? What if I proposed another sort of association or friendship, if you will," he heard himself saying.

She raised her brows. "Really, and what do you propose? I'm all ears, my lord."

"I do not think we ought to discuss it here. Is there no place we can go to be alone for a minute or two?" He glanced about the box, noting that the duchess had moved into another nearby and was animatedly talking to friends.

Paris did the same before shaking her head. "I do not think so, and we're alone for now. If you wish to say something to me, you best get to it."

Where the next words came from, Dominic would never know, but what he did know was he had to say something. Do something to make her be near him again. If he could only gain her friendship once more, then perhaps it could lead to what they once shared, what he had broken five years before.

"You are a widow with an heir. Your position in society

is secure. I thought that since you do not wish to marry, that may not mean that you would not consider other benefits that a gentleman could grant you." Dominic inwardly cringed that he was about to suggest what he was, but still, his shame would not halt what he was going to ask. He wanted her, only her, and he would do anything, be anything she wanted if it meant that he gained what *he* wanted.

"Other benefits, my lord?" She tilted her head, studying him. "What on earth could you possibly mean by such a suggestion?"

He leaned closer still to ensure privacy. "I'm suggesting that we become lovers. I satisfy your craving while you satisfy mine, so to speak."

"I have a craving?" she queried. "How would you know? We were only together once, and I do not remember it being anything so substantial that I should wish to do it again."

He cleared his throat, hoping that was not true and merely another spray of words to disarm him. "I do not know for certain, but from past exchanges with you, I had always thought you desired me long before you wished for me to be your husband. I do not think that has changed, no matter how mad you are at me still."

"Hmm," she said. "I am mad at you. That is true. You acted sinfully toward me, but your suggestion does intrigue me ..." She bit her lip, slipping it through her teeth, and heat licked along his spine. He had forgotten how much Paris tempted him during her first Season. Their kisses had been fire. Their one night was an encounter he dreamed of still. How he had made the choice he did, he would never understand. What a bastard he had been.

"I did enjoy my husband's attentions, and it is an element of marriage I do miss," she admitted.

He ground his teeth, pushing aside what conjured in his mind at her words. He would not dwell on whom she had been with, whom she'd enjoyed. She was here now, before him, and contemplating his offer. "Then use me, Paris. Be with me," he begged her. "Fuck me whenever you choose."

Her cheeks burned hotter at his words, yet her stomach twisted in delicious knots at the thought of being with Dominic. To her shame and as mad as she had been at him for years, that did not change the fact that she still wanted him in this way.

His idea intrigued her. He would be in her control, her power, and she could play him as well as he had played her. She knew what his goal would be. Seduce her into thinking she loved him still and wanted to marry him again. She would not.

She could be as callous and cold as he had been that afternoon in the Romney library and take what she wanted and leave him wanting more. In time she would break from him, wasting many weeks he could have courted another with no satisfaction from her, not concerning marriage in any case.

She had her own estates now, a London town house, and a son that secured the Hervey line. Her children were happy and healthy at their country estate, and there would be no chance of him meeting her daughter Maya. Should he do so, one look and he would know why she would not forgive him.

But there was no reason she could not take a little enjoyment from the only man who made her burn with the mere thought of him touching her. Punish him by taking what she wanted, getting satisfaction, and leaving him with none.

"You are very forward with your suggestion, my lord. I assume from your confidence that you believe you're more than capable of the position of my lover."

He glanced toward the stage as the theater staff snuffed the lights in the boxes for the second act. "I'm more than capable of making you enjoy yourself with me." He turned and met her eyes, and the determination she read in his hungry gaze left her breathless. "Let me make your Season enjoyable. It is the least that I can do." He picked up her gloved hand and kissed it, meeting her eyes as he did so.

Paris swallowed and found herself nodding. "Very well, my lord. I shall take you up on your offer, and we shall see if you indeed learned anything of bed sport while abroad."

He grinned and reminded her of the mischievous streak she once knew. "You will not regret it. I'll make sure of that." He stood. "Have a pleasant evening," he said and was gone.

Paris schooled her features, certain that the night was both pleasant and very much surprising. A turn of events she had not expected, but now looked forward to with more enthusiasm than she ought.

Careful, Paris. Do not lose your heart again.

She dismissed the thought, determined not to fail. Being intimate did not mean one had to lose one's heart. She would be careful to guard her emotions. It was only sex, after all, and she was no longer the naïve girl she had once been, and now Lord Astoridge would find out how true that was.

CHAPTER
SIX

The following evening Dominic pulled Paris into a waltz as soon as one started to play. He needed her in his arms, and now. It had been years since he had been so close to her, felt her womanly curves, and breathed in the delightful scent of lilies that always intoxicated him when she was near.

And now he had secured her agreement to be his lover. He wanted her, and soon. His body ached with the need to be with her, to have her in his arms, his to pleasure and enjoy. The thought of her speaking to him, of agreeing to his suggestion, left a heady ache in his groin that had not dissipated, not even when he had taken himself in hand.

"You appear very pleased with yourself, my lord," she said, looking up at him as he guided them about the dance floor.

He grinned and drank in her beauty. This evening she wore an abundance of diamonds in her hair that caught the candlelight as they danced, making her appear like a sparkling jewel.

His jewel he was determined to win again.

Not to mention her gown of copper tulle shimmered and hugged her womanly form, leaving very little to the imagination as to what lay beneath.

He wanted to get his hands on her body, honor and love it as she deserved. He wanted to hear her scream his name as he made her come.

"I have you speaking to me again. What is there not to be happy about?" he quipped. "There is no secret that behind all the finery and titles are just two people who find each other attractive. While we may not be as close as we once were, I am looking forward to seducing you," he whispered.

Her lips twitched before the slightest shrug lifted her shoulder. "You are very confident, my lord. I hope you do not disappoint."

"I will not, nor did I the last time, no matter what you say otherwise. I promise you that," he said, spinning them about before coming up the other side of the ballroom floor.

"There is one stipulation I require before we commence our illicit affair," she stated.

He watched her lips, and heat licked along his spine. He wanted to kiss her, here, now. "Anything," he said, willing to do whatever she wished, just so long as he got to taste her and soon.

"There is to be no kissing between us during our exchanges."

Dominic stumbled in the dance. "Apologies," he said, quickly gaining his feet. "I long to kiss you, Paris. Why can we not do so?" He fought to keep the disappointment and the longing from his tone but failed miserably.

"It is too intimate, I believe. I do not want you to think more of an interlude than what it is. A way for us both to enjoy each other, give each other pleasure with nothing else expected from the situation."

"I want to kiss you," he admitted. "I've wanted to kiss you from the very first moment I saw you again but days ago."

She shook her head, her attention shifting from him. "It is too personal. The deal is off if you cannot agree to this."

"I promise not to fall in love with you even if we do," he teased, hoping to change her mind. How could he make love to her, bring her to the heights of pleasure, and not kiss her sweet lips? "Please do not deny me this," he begged shamefully.

"If you do not agree to what I want, there will be nothing else between us, Lord Astoridge. Do you concur or not?" she demanded of him, her determination easy to read in her eyes.

He sighed, knowing there was little left to say, not that it would stop him from trying to change her mind. In time he may persuade her to kiss him. "Very well, I agree to what you wish, but I can kiss you anywhere else. Will you agree to that?"

"Of course. I look forward to where you think I may like being kissed."

His cock hardened, and he inwardly groaned at the thought of where he wanted to kiss, to lave and bring her to orgasm. "I could think of a few locations. I'm not certain you may know, but I would like to show you."

She chuckled, her eyes alight with mirth. "Oh, Lord Astoridge, there is nothing you can do to me that has not been done already. Lord Hervey was a passionate man, and I enjoyed my bed sport with him since we're being so very forward with each other."

"The thought of you being intimate with anyone makes my blood run cold. I do not like you mentioning it."

"Really," she said, surprise crossing her pretty face. "Well, perhaps you ought to have thought of that before you threw me over for an heiress which ..." She frowned, looking about. "I've yet to see you marry. Is there a reason why you did not? Do not tell me you pined for me all these years, for I would not believe it. I know your reputation was as wild and dissolute in France as it was here before you courted me. How is it that you never married?"

Dominic was unsure himself why he had not. Not that he had not had several chances in Paris society to court and marry an eligible young lady who would have suited his stipulations and his mother's lofty ideals. But each time he came close to proposing, Paris's face had fluttered in his mind, taunting him as the one whom he had lost, and the words had never come forth.

"The ladies that I courted were not right. Not in the end. There was always something missing that I could not locate, no matter how hard I tried to make myself speak the words I must."

"I feel for them then. I hope you did not lead them on a merry dance like you did me. That would be cruel and unfair, and I do not wish to hear of anyone else suffering from your haughty ideals."

"I never courted anyone in the way that I pursued you. I danced and had supper, even attended several dinner party events in Paris over the years, but I never overstepped the bounds of propriety as I did with you."

. . .

P aris met his eyes and could see he was sincere, and yet still, a part of her wanted to hurt him. To taunt his conscience over how relentlessly he pursued her until he did not. That he had been like a beautiful summer's day one minute and drenching, cold rain the next.

So changeable. So hurtful in his steadfast ways.

"And yet, in truth, you never did anything to me that society would not approve of. They do not know that you took liberties you should not have, or that I allowed them. You left, and I married another. No harm done. Is that not correct? You were a gentleman in every outward way one could be, but when we were alone, the way you spoke gave me hope. The way you touched me told me you wanted me as your wife. I hope you did not do the same abroad to any more innocent, naïve women." Paris wanted him to feel as if she were putting his morals under question, as her right. He did ruin her and left her to rot. Not that he had known their one night had left her pregnant, but *she* did, and he would pay for the hurt he caused her.

"I never did any such thing. Not with any of the young ladies, I promise you," he declared.

His words made warmth settle where she had become so used to cold and aloofness. She was glad he had not rutted his way around France, but then, nor should she care.

"If we're to engage in anything between us, there are rules that will need to be obeyed. Not only is there no kissing, but we shall not spend the night together. You must leave, and so must I when we've engaged with each other at our respective homes. We're not to engage in anything at balls and parties other than dances such as this. And you are to court and find a woman who will suit you as a wife. I do not want to stand in the way of you finding someone to marry." With him courting another, it would stop her from falling too hard at his feet once again. Not kissing Dominic, not becoming emotionally entangled with him, would protect her and be best for them both.

Their time had passed. She had married another and had a wonderful child who would carry on her husband's name and a daughter to fill her heart. Lord Astoridge needed to do the same with anyone who was not her.

"You want me to court another while we're sleeping together?" he asked, pulling her close, his large hand slipping across her back and making her skin prickle in awareness.

"Yes, that is what I wish. I do not feel anything for you, Lord Astoridge. Nothing at all. You must not think that I do merely because I'm willing to be your lover."

He stared at her, his mouth agape before he snapped it closed. "You do not feel anything for me at all? I do not believe it, not if we're to partake in what we're discussing, my lady," he argued, a small frown marring his brow.

"It is what it is, my lord. It has been five years, and so much has happened since you went away. Of course I do not feel anything for you and wish you to have what I did with Lord Hervey. I'm not completely unfeeling, but I do not want you to look for something between us when there will never be any emotional attachment from me to you again."

He cleared his throat, and for several turns, they waltzed about the ballroom floor without talking. She could see he was mulling over her words, debating arguing further if his thinned lips were any indication, but in the end, he sighed, and she knew she had won this war at least.

"Very well. I shall agree to all that you state, but you

cannot stop me from hoping that in time I may be able to win back your trust and mayhap your heart."

Paris smiled but shook her head. "I do not think that shall ever happen, my lord. If there is one thing that has changed about me in the last five years it is that I'm more independent and stubborn than I ever was before. I know what I do and do not want, and another husband, for all their value, is not something I wish for. I'm content in my life, hence why I shall take a lover, but nothing more. You will fail in your quest if you do try," she said, seeing only determination light in his brown gaze.

"Let the games begin, my lady."

She chuckled. "If you say so, my lord."

CHAPTER
SEVEN

The following evening Dominic sat in the supper room alone at Lord and Lady Smithfield's ball and watched as the Countess of Hervey flirted outrageously with Lord Bankes, an earl from Somerset.

He spooned the syllabub into his mouth, his attention steadfast on the countess as she laughed and every so often reached out and touched the earl's arm as they spoke.

That the earl, a man five years older than himself, was rich and had an abundant, extravagant estate in Somerset only worsened the unwavering nerves that twisted in his stomach.

He ought to join them, throw himself between them in a way, but he did not. She did not want him interfering in her life, and he only had himself to blame for her coolness toward him in social situations.

But when would he get her alone? His body burned to have her in his arms. He wanted to kiss her, even though she had forbidden such intimate actions, but he was certain he could persuade her otherwise. Change her mind about not becoming emotionally involved with him.

How could she not? How could either of them remain aloof when being so intimate with each other?

She was deluding herself, not that he would tell her so, but he would enjoy proving her wrong until she admitted the truth.

"You look as if you're about to commit murder," Lord Lupton-Gage said, sitting beside him and glancing in the direction he watched.

"Ah, I see what has caught your eye." His friend's chuckle grated on Dominic's nerves, and he glared at him. "Have you had any success in winning her friendship back, if not anything else?" he asked him.

Dominic knew better than to disclose what he had arranged with Paris, but even so, he would have loved to reveal and debate what he could do to win her back.

Well, he supposed he could do the latter.

"She will be hard to win, I fear," he admitted. "I shall have my work cut out for me. That is a certainty. But also, it shall be well worth the wait when she is mine once more."

Lupton-Gage smiled at his wife, who strolled past on her way back to the ballroom with the Marchioness of Chilsten. "I find that when my wife is stubborn, I must seduce her to see my way of things."

Dominic snorted, certain that the Marchioness of Lupton-Gage was no pushover, just like the Countess of Hervey was not. "Do not give advice that you yourself cannot follow through on, Gage."

His friend chuckled. "Very well, your words may hold some truth, but what else do you have to select from?"

"Friendship, I suppose, even if the thought of only ever being friends with Lady Hervey makes my stomach churn. I regret the choice I made five years ago, and I wish I could take it back, but I cannot, and now I fear there is no future, as she says." Not to mention that he had lied to her and was hiding his financial predicament that he could only keep from others for so long. Eventually, it would become known that he was struggling to pay for everything his family required for the Season. Already he had a drawer full of unpaid accounts and promises to those suppliers.

"Well, if she does not want a husband, why not look elsewhere? You cannot force a woman to return to what she once was. In time people change," Gage mentioned, his eyes on his wife, who stood beside Paris and the Duchess of Romney.

"Lady Lupton-Gage's feelings did not seem to change no matter how long you were apart."

"No, they did not," he agreed. "But not everyone is the same, and from what I understand, Lady Hervey was happy in her marriage. Maybe you ought to look elsewhere, do as she states. From my position, it does not look like she wants you in that way."

His friend's words were hard to swallow, and he downed his wine, watching Paris as Lord Bankes escorted her onto the dance floor. She did appear happier than he expected. She did not seem to care at all that he was here while he had been watching from afar and all but pining for the woman.

Maybe Gage was right. Maybe he ought to court another and strive to marry for wealth. That did not mean he would not get affection from the union.

"I think you are right. I will look to pursue a woman who is agreeable to a union with myself." And if Lady Hervey so happens to want to enjoy bed sport with him in the interim, then all the better for it. But he would not chase her like some besotted fool who could not remove her from his mind.

He was no burr. He was a viscount, a lord of the realm, not some lovesick fool pining for a woman who did not want him.

Determined, he turned to Lord Lupton-Gage. "I'm off then. I see Lady Esme is standing beside her mama and is all alone. I shall go and speak to her, ask her to dance. It is time that I settled, and she will do well enough."

Gage raised his brow. "Do try at least to fall in love with your wife. It will make the union all the better for it, trust me," he said.

Dominic stood and made his way toward her. She caught sight of him and blushed prettily. He bowed before her and her mama. "Lady Esme, would you do me the honor of dancing with me?" he asked her.

She glanced at her mother before gifting him with a smile that lit up her face. She was a pretty woman with similar color hair as Lady Hervey, not to mention her eyes were blue as well. He swallowed. Surely the similarities were not knowingly done on his behalf. He was not such a fool to pick the one women in London who looked most like Paris.

"I would be honored, my lord," she said, taking his hand.

He led her onto the floor for a waltz and shook off the doubts that plagued him. Lady Esme was beautiful, wealthy, and perfectly suitable. It did not matter she was not Paris Smith.

Did not matter at all.

Paris did not know what was wrong with her, but the sight of Lord Astoridge dancing and playing the merry bachelor, the suave, charming lord toward Lady

Esme, made her teeth ache. No doubt from the sweetness he seemed to be bestowing on the heiress.

Was he taking her up on her advice and courting another? She hoped he was. It was for the best since he was long overdue to marry and have an heir. She had already done all of those things, and happily so, she did not want to be beholden to another husband again.

Not even the handsome rouge Viscount Astoridge.

So why did the sight of his lordship dancing and chortling with the Lady Esme irritate her so? She was an heiress and would suit him perfectly in that sense, at least.

"You appear ruffled," Millie said at her side, passing her a glass of champagne. "I did not think you wanted anything to do with Lord Astoridge."

Paris shook her head and took a long sip of her wine. "I do not. That has not changed, but I suppose the fact that he has returned and is now courting an heiress aggravates me. I do not understand why some gentlemen think that is the most important factor in a marriage. Lord Hervey did not think so."

"The exemplary Lord Hervey, may his soul rest in peace, was a special kind of gentleman, and adored you."

Paris narrowed her eyes. Did her friend's words mean she did not believe Lord Astoridge cared for her as much as her husband had? All true, she supposed, since he found it so easy to reject her that hurtful afternoon.

"Your Grace, Miss Smith, a lovely ball, is it not?" the Dowager Viscountess Astoridge said, joining them and smiling toward the gathered throng.

Paris heard Millie choke on her beverage, and Paris stared down at the older woman with distaste. She wasn't fooled enough not to know a lot of Dominic's past decisions were made because of the meddling, social climbing matron at her side.

"Lady Astoridge, it is very good to see you, but you are mistaken," Millie said when she had recovered her decorum. "My good friend Lady Hervey has not been Miss Smith for several years. Have you forgotten she married the Earl of Hervey?" she asked her.

The older woman threw back her head and laughed as if the duchess had made an amusing witticism. "Oh, of course. I forget, you see. I do apologize. You have not been part of society for so long. I all but forgot you existed until I saw you here this evening." The older woman's lips thinned into a displeased line. "The same evening and ball that my son Lord Astoridge is attending. How providential."

Paris bit back the caustic retort she wanted to spill and instead smiled. "Maybe your memory is a little hazy, my lady. I was not the one who left England for five years. I have been here all the time and am part of this society. Lord and Lady Smithfield are good friends. I would not miss their yearly ball, not for anything," she said, trying to keep her tone aloof, but from the little muscle that worked in the viscountess's jaw feared she had failed.

"Of course," Lady Astoridge stated. "But my son was a favorite of yours, was he not? I hope you do not favor him still, as I fear your heart may be bruised a second time. Especially since he has shown great interest in Lady Esme. I'm sure you remember her since you married the man she was rumored to love." Her ladyship turned and watched her son and dance partner for several moments. "If you do speak to him, I hope you help me in my quest for him to marry. She is simply perfect for him," she said, tapping Paris on the arm with her fan.

Paris narrowed her eyes, and something bitter and

resentful snapped inside of her. "Of course, my lady. I shall do all I can to help Lord Astoridge make his choice," she mumbled as her ladyship left her.

"Do I dare ask what that was all about?" Millie questioned.

Paris shook her head. "Not at all. It is not worth your worry," she answered, looking out at the dance floor. The pit of her stomach clenched at the sight of Dominic watching her.

He could court whomever he wanted, but that did not mean she would not take her pound of flesh, make him fall in love with her as she had him, and then break his heart as he had hers. Her revenge may be cruel and unnecessary, but scorned she most definitely was, and it was time she had her retribution.

CHAPTER
EIGHT

Dominic watched as Paris excused herself from her party and strolled toward the terrace. He glanced about the room and followed her, satisfied that no one was watching him.

Stepping out onto the large, square flagstones, he caught sight of her golden tulle gown slipping about a darkened corner. The chill of the air caught him off guard as he closed the door, understanding why no one else was outside this evening, preferring the indoors.

He hurried about the corner and found Paris seated on a stone seat, looking up at the moonless night.

"Are you feeling well?" he asked her, coming to stand at her side.

"Your mother still dislikes me as much as she ever had. Do you know she called me Miss Smith this evening as if to remind me of my humble beginnings? Not that such an insult had the reaction she would have liked. If anything, it only makes me more determined to vex her further by my presence."

"My apologies, Paris. She can be difficult at times."

She stood and walked up to him, watching him with an intentness that left him on edge and made the blood in his veins quicken. "I'm proud of my family and my little town of Grafton. Your mother is a snob and forgets that I now rank higher than her in society and that I can make her life difficult should she continue to try to insult me. I suggest you keep her in line, lest she finds herself uninvited to balls and parties she holds so highly in her life."

Dominic swallowed and inwardly swore. He did not need his mother warning off Paris, being so rude to a woman who did not deserve it. If anyone found out that they were penniless and on the verge of losing all that they owned, the invitations would soon dry up. It was friends like Paris, Lord Lupton-Gage, and others who could keep the wolves from the door should he need to ask for help.

Not that he could do such a thing, he would rather marry Lady Esme than stoop to that level. Or better yet, convince Paris that she was angry with him, yes, but that she still loved him, wanted him.

Their passionate agreement told him that she still wanted him, and that gave him hope.

"I will speak to her," he said.

Paris studied him a moment before she stepped near him, her hands slipping down the front of his superfine coat. An expense he could ill afford, but required for the Season.

Her touch made the breath in his lungs hitch, and he swallowed the need that coursed through him. "I do not like to be told what to do, Dominic. I like to do and say whatever I wish and be accountable to no one. I want to enjoy my Season and not be insulted by women who no longer hold power over me and my poor past self." She tapped his chest, a wistful smile playing on her kissable lips. "Do not let her insult me again, or our deal is off."

Fire coursed through his blood and he clasped her about the waist, wrenching her close. "If I do as you say, which I will, I promise you, will you let me kiss you now?" he all but begged her, inwardly cringing from how much he wanted her, needed her.

How he had survived so many years without her in France, he could not fathom. He was a bastard to have wanted a second chance, and he deserved her reserve. She owed him nothing.

"I do not think so. No kisses or anything more, not this evening, at least." She patted his chest, pushing him away. "I will let you know when I wish to pursue our agreement. Do be patient." She stepped out of his hold and strolled back toward the terrace doors, leaving him in the darkness.

He ran a hand through his hair. His body alight with unsated need. It had been months since he had been with a woman, and even then, the lady was paid for her time.

But to have Paris warm his bed, her long, strawberry locks spread over his pillows, her willing, womanly curves his to cherish and savor ... He ground his teeth, fighting the urge to follow her, steal a kiss, and seduce her to being with him now.

Would she relent? Would she succumb to his charms? He was so out of practice he doubted she would.

With a sigh, he returned to the ball and partook in several wines before seeking out Lady Esme for a second dance. If he could not have Paris, he would at least attempt to make her jealous in the interim.

. . .

The following morning Paris took one of the horses and grooms and rode down to Hyde Park. A brisk, early morning ride was just what she needed to clear her head after the ball the night before.

Well, to be truthful, her interaction with Lord Astoridge. It had taken all her power not to succumb to his charms. His heartfelt words and need that all but oozed from his very soul.

She had heard such promises before. Had fallen for the words men's lying lips spilled.

When Lord Hervey had asked her to marry him, but days after Lord Astoridge had thrown her over, she knew she could not refuse. He was her savior, a man who wanted her for herself and did not care that she came with nothing.

Men such as Dominic glittered, and people naturally gravitated toward them. But just because someone sparkled and was fetching did not mean they were the same inwardly.

Paris arrived at Rotten Row and was glad to see only a handful of people using the track. She walked along its edge, happy to merely be out and enjoying the brisk morning ride. Several riders cantered past, and she waved when they called out welcome to her before the thumping of horses' hooves sounded closer than they ought.

"I thought it was you," Lord Astoridge said, pulling his horse up alongside hers. Paris inwardly sighed at the sight that he made. His cravat loosely tied about his neck gave a glimpse of his chest beneath. His windswept hair fell over his brow, and the shadow of stubble on his jaw all but screamed rake.

Men should not be allowed to be so handsome. Especially men who had broken women's hearts and deserved no praise. "Lord Astoridge. You are up early this morning," she said, pushing her horse forward.

He chuckled, the deep sound making her innards tremble. How could she still react to him this way after all he had done to her? Curse her weak heart for reveling in his presence.

"I enjoy a good, hard ride in the morning," he said, a wicked glint in his eyes.

She shook her head, not succumbing to his naughtiness. "That is good, I suppose," she said, looking and noting that other than three riders well ahead of them, they were quite alone. "I needed to clear my head. Today I have many calls to make along with this evening's costume ball at the Duncannons. Are you attending?" she asked him.

He nodded. "I am. I'm going to go as Caesar. A distant relative from what my father once proclaimed, although no one in my family has ever confirmed such suspicions."

"So you'll be wearing a dress like myself," she teased, unable to not picture what he would look like wearing a toga. Would she gain a glimpse of his knees and portions of his thighs? Were they as muscular as she remembered them?

The thought made heat pool between her legs, and she cursed herself for succumbing to his charms. She should not. He did not deserve her regard, but he was so tempting how could she not want what she had once coveted?

What he had offered her only nights ago. She studied him, drank in his handsome profile and kissable mouth, and thought more on the matter.

"I will be," he answered, his voice dripping in insinuation. "What of you? Who will you be arriving as?" he asked.

Paris shrugged, not willing to disclose everything to him so soon, and besides, she wasn't sure at all what she would wear. She had several outfits to choose from. "That you will have to wait and see, my lord," she said, fighting back a grin, knowing that wasn't so very true. Her costume of Cleopatra had been chosen days before.

"I look forward to seeing very well," he drawled. They rode again in silence for several steps before he said, "Have you given any more thought to my suggestion to you the other night?"

She raised her brow, feigning ignorance. "I do not know what you mean?" His lips twitched, and she knew he read through her words.

"I mean about you and I becoming lovers. I want you in my bed. I do not know how much clearer I need to make things."

The thought made her blood sing, and from her body's reaction to his words, she wanted him too. To hurt and punish him, yes, but also to take pleasure. To enjoy the company of a man in such an intimate space. It had been so very long, over a year, since she had been with anyone and her body craved to be touched, kissed, and every other delicious thing a man could do to a woman.

"Oh, that." She laughed, shrugging. "I may need to wait and see what you're willing to do first. This evening at the Duncannons, meet me in the music room. It is several doors down from the ballroom. There we shall discuss the matter further, and I shall see if you're truly committed."

"I'm dedicated, Paris," he stated, meeting her eye, and something dark and hungry that she read in his brown eyes told her he was.

CHAPTER
NINE

T he Duncannons had outdone themselves with the decorations for the costume ball. Hundreds of guests were in attendance, the ballroom packed to the brim with people from throughout history. Some less favorable than others. Paris could see Henry VIII and his wife Anne Boleyn, the poor chit hopefully would have a better evening than the real lady herself had in life.

"What fun this night is to be," Millie stated at her side. Dressed this evening as Marie de' Medici, although she looked like so many other French queens who strolled the ballroom floor.

"I find costume balls so amusing that one cannot help but have a pleasant evening," she said. Paris glanced about the room and could not see Dominic in attendance.

She hoped he would not be long, if only so she could see him in a toga. But that wasn't the only reason why. She wanted him in her bed too. Not that she had forgiven him his sins against her, but merely to appease an ache that had begun in her that would not relent.

She would never forgive him for his treatment of her,

but he was the only man who had ever made her burn with desire, and she needed to feel alive again.

Not to mention to make him fall in love with her, give him hope so she may rip it from beneath him when he least expected it.

The thought made her giddy, and she clasped two crystal glasses of champagne from a passing footman and handed one to Millie.

"To the costume ball. May we have a jolly good time," she toasted.

Millie clinked her glass against Paris's, and they both took a healthy sip. "I think your Mark Antony is here," Millie said, nodding toward the ballroom door.

Paris glanced in the direction of the doors and felt her mouth gape. "That's not Mark Antony. That's Caesar," she said, not wanting anyone to think she had dressed as Caesar's love interest. She frowned, hating the idea that people's tongues may wag, and regretted her costume immediately.

"Well, your Roman gentleman seems to be making his way over to you in any case," Millie said, tapping her glass against hers a second time before sauntering off.

Paris whispered for her to come back but to no avail. Her friend ignored her plea and moved on to another group of friends. Paris inwardly swore. Watching Lord Astoridge stroll toward her with a determination that left her breathless was not what she needed.

She needed to remain angry at him. Not allow the handsomeness that oozed from his every pore to seduce her to forget how he treated her.

He may be all gentlemanly behavior now, but that was not always the case. Because of his cruelty, her daughter would never know who her birth father was.

"My queen," he said, dipping into a low bow before her, his eyes sparkling with mischief when he stood.

She raised her brows and attempted to look less than impressed. Not that anyone could not be impressed with his costume. Historically accurate toga right down to his leather sandals.

Her attention dipped to his feet, his bare, muscular calves and knees. He was as hairy as she remembered, and God save her sinful soul, she wondered if he wore anything under that silk but himself.

"Caesar. Still alive, I see," she drawled.

"That I am." He chuckled and came to stand at her side. "You look beautiful, Paris," he said, his attention moving over her like a caress. She felt every shifting of his gaze from the tip of her nose to her feet. "When I saw you this evening, I felt my breath catch."

Paris threw back her head and laughed, a part of her reveling in his attention, his sweet, seductive words, while another part of her, a dark, angry portion of her soul, wanted to growl that he dared even speak to her.

"You are so very good with words, my lord. You remind me of the man I once knew. A man willing to say anything so long as he gained his way or pleasure," she whispered. "Before moving on to greener pastures."

He flinched at her words, and a small frown deepened between his eyes. "Can we not throw barbs at each other this evening? I know I did you wrong, but you married well despite my atrocious behavior against you. I know we shared one sinful night, but nothing came of it."

Paris bit down her retort that something did come of them sleeping together. A beautiful, sweet girl who had been denied her true name because of the disregard of the man before her. But she could not tell him that. To do so would ruin Maya, and no matter how angry or hurt she was, she could not injure her child.

"Very well, I shall lay down my sword, which is probably best. I would hate for Caesar to be murdered again by a knife in the back," she said, only half-teasingly.

He grinned, watching her. "Shall we dance?" he asked, holding out his hand.

She reluctantly slipped her hand into his and let him lead her onto the floor. The orchestra started to play a waltz, and soon she was floating about the floor in her white silk tunic, all that separated her and Dominic.

His hand felt warm and large on her back, the thin material no barrier to his heated touch. Her skin prickled, and a shiver stole down her spine. How easy it would be to fall for such charms again. But she could not. They were not for her. He would best be dancing with Lady Esme.

As if the reflection of the one woman who loathed her most in society was conjured at the thought, she noted her on the side of the ballroom floor, watching them. Her pinched mouth told Paris without words that she did not like Lord Astoridge dancing with her.

"Lady Esme will hate me even more now that you're dancing with me. You should spend more time with her, rather than wasting it with me."

"I do not want Lady Esme in my bed," he stated. "There is only one woman who interests me right at this moment, and I'm holding her in my arms."

"Still so very good with words, Lord Astoridge," she said, forgetting she had promised to be civil.

He stared at her, nonplussed. "Play nice, Paris," he warned.

"And if I do not wish to?" she replied, feeling as though

the conversation had slipped into another subject entirely and one that was not at all proper.

"Then I shall have to punish you, my queen," he stated. "As a Roman senator, it is my duty, I feel, to guide you when I believe you're misguided in your thinking."

She scoffed, wondering if he were ever so arrogant when she had known him years ago. She did not think so. "Punish me? And how are you supposed to do that?" she questioned, heat pooling between her thighs.

She was wicked and wrong, but she had also been without a man for so long that she ached. Better the devil one knew than the one not known.

"You did not specify a time when we should meet in the music room this evening. Tell me when and I shall reveal all," he said, fighting to keep his cock from standing to attention.

The toga was no good under such circumstances, and the last thing he wanted to do was walk around with his cock hard and poking out of his costume like some randy dog.

Which, in truth, he was. It had been so very long since he had been with a woman. The thought of having Paris, of stripping her bare of her tunic, of taking his fill of her body made sweat break out on his upper lip.

"Before supper," she said, meeting his eyes.

He read the fire that burned in her blue gaze, his own a conflagration also. The waltz came to an end, and he swept her to a stop. "Until then, my queen," he said, reluctantly letting her go.

She turned on her sandaled feet and left him to watch her stroll away, as regal as Queen Cleopatra herself.

He beat down the desire that raged through him. Of thoughts of having her alone, his to make love to, and only in a matter of hours. He could win her back yet. The thought of courting Lady Esme was not something he could continue. The lady deserved better than what he could offer her, and he would forever want another.

The remainder of the evening dragged, even when he had offered to dance with several ladies, including Lady Esme, whom he could not cut. That would never do, and he was no longer the immature youth he had once been.

Even so, he did not give any of them an idea of his interest being any more than that of an acquaintance, and with any fortune, Lady Esme would soon realize the same.

He stood near the supper room doors, watching where the ladies left to head to the retiring room. He glimpsed a woman in white silk slip through the door, and he knew Paris had left for their rendezvous.

He downed the last of his brandy and went after her, slipping out of the ballroom doors before making his way to the music room.

He found her sitting on the piano stool, facing the door. She leaned back against the instrument, the hood of the pianoforte down so as to stop it from making music.

The moonlight shone in through the doors, and Paris looked like a goddess from the past.

"Close the door and lock it," she instructed him.

He did as she bade, striding toward her with determined steps. His cock hardened, and he stood before her, not attempting to hide how she made him feel.

She looked up at him, mischief in her eyes. "You said you would punish me, but I do not think a Roman senator has such power over a queen, so I think there is something else you should do for your monarch."

He took a calming breath, nodding. "Anything you desire. I'm your humble servant," he said, playing along with her game.

"Mmmm, well, let us see," she purred. "I think you ought to get down on your knees and beg for forgiveness. I think I deserve such groveling," she said, the determination in her eyes telling him she was in earnest.

His pride growled at the idea, but he relented and did as she commanded. She watched him, spreading her legs wide.

"Earn my forgiveness, Lord Astoridge," his queen commanded. "I think you can understand in what way I want."

CHAPTER

TEN

P aris took a calming breath and fought not to blush, not to stop this madness she was about to embark on.

She sat on the piano stool, watching with much antici-pation, along with the satisfaction of seeing Dominic on his knees before her.

She leaned forward, lifting his chin when he did as she bade. "Now that you're before me on bended knee, I think you ought to ask for forgiveness before we continue anything else."

He leaned toward her, trying to capture her lips, and she shook her head. "No, no, no, my lord. No kissing, remember?" she said, placing a finger on his lips.

He sighed but pulled back in agreement. "My queen," he stated.

"No," she said, stopping him. "Not my queen. Paris is my name." She needed to hear him use her given name, not some make-believe, dress-up name for this evening.

He cleared his throat. "Paris, please forgive me for what I did to you. I was young and foolish and did not know what I was doing. I let others guide me, and I should not have done that to you. You deserved so much more than what I offered. Allow me to make it up to you tonight. Let me give you pleasure instead of pain."

She swallowed hard the lump in her throat that formed at the sound of his apology. Nothing he did or said could make her forgive him for the wrong he did, not only on her behalf, but that of her daughter too, she reminded herself. A youth or not, he ought to have known better.

Play the game, Paris. Teach him a lesson in love that he will never forget ...

Determination coursed through her, and she rallied. She would play this game of seduction, take what she wanted, give him hope, and then strip him of it when he least expected it.

Revenge was a cruel mistress, and Lord Astoridge was about to discover how cruel she could be.

"Your apology is accepted, my lord," she said, leaning back again on the pianoforte.

He met her eye, and she shivered at the determination, the desire that burned within his gaze. He reached out, his large hands clasping the hem of her tunic.

She swallowed as he bit his lip, slipping the silk of her gown over her knees to reveal her thighs. "So damn beautiful," he whispered, pushing her legs wider. "You have no idea how much I have dreamed of being with you again. Of having you in my bed."

Paris bit her lip as he slipped her gown about her hips, exposing her to his hungry gaze. He dipped his head, brushing his lips against the skin on her thigh, paying attention to the sensitive flesh beside her knees.

She sighed, clasping the piano stool with determination to stop from reaching for Dominic.

"Damn, I want you so much," he admitted, sliding his tongue along the inside of one leg before he came to her mons. He slipped her legs over his shoulders and pulled her against his mouth.

She gasped as his tongue slipped between her folds, laving her cunny with a hunger that left her reeling. His mouth moved on her with ravenous strokes, flicking and delving into her with relentless perfection.

Paris fought not to moan, not to cry out at the exquisiteness of his touch. Over and over, she reminded herself they were at a ball. No place to be so bold, but nor could she ignore what he did to her.

Her body was alight with need. Moisture pooled at her aching core, and the sweet sense of satisfaction slowly edged ever closer with each lick, each flick of his tongue.

"Oh yes," she breathed, fisting his locks into her hands.

He growled against her quim, moving his hand to touch her there. His finger sank into her, filling her as he once had, and she moaned. "I want my cock where my hand is," he admitted.

She looked down and watched him slowly take her with his finger, in and out in glorious repetition that left her incapable of speech. She licked her lips, wanting the same, but not tonight. This night was for him to do as she wished. To give her pleasure. She would be damned if she would waver with her plan and give him satisfaction too.

"Soon," she promised.

He dipped his head, his strokes with his hand increasing, thrusting deep, sweet pleasure that taunted her to no end. She closed her eyes as his mouth came down on her again. He suckled her nubbin, and it was too much.

Waves of pleasure crashed over her, and she rode his hand and face, took what she wanted, and allowed the delight to thrum through her until she was weightless with fulfillment.

"You taste wicked and sweet," he said, wringing out every ounce of her orgasm. "I'm so fucking hard," he admitted, taking himself in hand.

She sat forward, slipping her legs off his shoulders, and pushed him back. Her dress settled about her legs as if they had not just partaken in something utterly scandalous. "I thank you for your service, my lord. I do so hope we get to do this again. It was most enjoyable." Paris stood and stepped past him.

She heard him stumble upright before he wrenched her to a stop at the door. "Paris, where are you going? I thought ..."

She patted his chest before tidying up his toga, which had crumpled a little from their rendezvous. "You thought what, my lord?" she asked, wanting to hear him say the words aloud.

He frowned and ran a hand through his hair. The confusion on his handsome face made her anger falter, but a moment before, she remembered why she loathed him still.

"It is nothing," he said, seemingly understanding that she was to receive pleasure but no one else this evening.

Paris pushed down the guilt that rose at her actions. The words that two wrongs did not make a right ran through her mind. But was that entirely true? She was a woman, and they were the sex that always earned the worst part of any bargain. Why could she not come out on top, for this night at least?

"You best return first, and I shall follow you in several minutes. We do not wish to get caught together. I know how much that would displease you."

Paris turned on her slippered feet, unlocked the door,

and fled. Were his words a little affront toward how she had treated him this evening? Letting her know that he understood that she had used him to get what she wanted? Just as he had used her before leaving without a backward glance.

Instead of returning to the ball, she climbed the stairs to use the retiring room. Thankfully the space was empty, and she strode to a window and wrenched it open, breathing deep the cool, night air.

She could do this. She could remain aloof and unaffected by him. Use him and hurt him. She could. She had to.

Did she not?

D ominic ran a hand over his mouth and breathed deeply. What the hell had just happened? Never in his life had a woman used him in the manner that Paris had, not without returning the favor.

He shut the music room door and leaned against it, needing to clear his mind and ease the pounding in his chest.

Had she used him? Ordered him to do as she pleased with no intention of giving him satisfaction in return?

A little part of him marveled at her gumption and the callous use of him. Men used women for such things all the time, but to have it turned against him, a lord, no matter his dire financial situation, was a heady temptation indeed.

By God, he wanted her even more now.

He wanted her to use him up. To command him to do as she wished. To make her come on his face, his cock, on top or beneath him. He would take her any way she would gift her pretty, delectable self and be happy.

He strode over to a window and wrenched it open,

breathing the crisp night air deeply. He needed to get a hold of himself. He could not leave this room until the tent under his toga dissipated, and he needed to go home, if only so he could wrench off at the thought of her.

The night air went some way in bringing his pulse back to a normal rhythm, and he took a calming breath. The thought of seeing her again, of being with her alone such as they were this evening, was not enough.

Should he call on her tomorrow afternoon after the "at homes" were concluded for the morning? Would he be able to seduce her into some other romp, such as the one they had enjoyed this evening?

He reached for his cock, stroking it, fighting the urge to spend in a potted plant nearby. He wasn't that lowly or vulgar, but heavens above, this evening Paris had shown another side to her that left him reeling.

A side he liked very much and one he could use to his advantage.

CHAPTER ELEVEN

Paris thanked the last of her guests who visited her 'at home' before slumping onto her settee in the drawing room and taking a deep breath.

Her first social function at home went well, and she was pleased so many of her peers came to see her. Including Millie, who had asked her about the night before relentlessly and where she had scuttled off to just before supper.

Not that she would say too much on that matter. She did not know herself what it all meant, and if she had stepped too far down a particular road and could not now turn about and change her mind.

"Lord Astoridge is here to see you, my lady. Would you like me to send him away?" her butler Frederick asked in a quieter tone so his lordship could not hear.

Paris stared at the unlit hearth and sat up straight. She glanced at the time, wondering why he would be here so late. "You may send his lordship in, thank you," she said, not entirely sure what she would say to Dominic upon seeing him again.

Everything was different now. Her plan to punish him no longer sat well with her conscience.

It was cruel to use another person. She knew that better than most. So to turn around and punish someone with the same intention to cause hurt seemed wrong.

She glanced up at the mantel and spotted the two small miniatures of her children, and a little of her apprehension ceased. Her daughter had been so close to becoming a bastard. A young woman who would never have everything that she now did thanks to Lord Hervey.

No. No matter how ill her plan sat on her soul, Lord Astoridge deserved a little comeuppance.

"Lady Hervey," a deep baritone said from the door before the snick of the door closing, locking them away together, clicked loud in the room.

"Lord Astoridge, I did not expect you today," she said, leaning forward and pouring two cups of tea. Without asking, she placed one cube of sugar and a dash of cream, just as he liked it.

He sat in the wingback chair, crossing his long legs before holding out his hand to take the tea. "Thank you," he said, sipping. "You did not forget, I see."

Paris secured her cup and sat back on the settee, pausing to answer. "A good hostess remembers how all her friends take their tea."

"Friends? Is that what we are, Paris?" he asked her.

She shrugged, wondering if they were herself. "Enemies too, I suppose."

His eyes narrowed, and he studied her a moment. Paris fought not to fidget and ask him what his inspection of her meant. What he was doing here in the privacy of her own home when she had not sent for him. Had not asked him to rendezvous with her this afternoon.

"What happened last evening?" he asked.

She chuckled to hide the heat that kissed her cheeks at his query. "I believe it was quite obvious what occurred, my lord. Do not tell me you cannot remember when you're alone with a woman like we were."

"I know what physically happened, Paris, but I want to know why I had the impression you were taunting me. Teasing me with no inclination to share the enjoyment."

Paris sipped her tea. She would not tell him that their time together last evening had sent her reeling. That she, too, had returned home, disheveled and out of sorts. Satisfied and yet not.

"We were at a ball. There is not always time for both parties to find satisfaction," she answered. "Next time, mayhap we both shall come to a gratifying conclusion."

"You have changed," he said at length. "You are not as carefree and sweet as you once were. I suppose I only have myself to blame for that. And if I do not, then you most certainly will."

"Can you blame me?" she bit back, unwilling to be this story's villain. "I gave myself to you, and you cast me aside like some whore you had found deficient. I went from seeing you, talking and kissing you most nights to being left alone, given the cut direct before all the *ton*. Lord Hervey saw your treatment of me and offered his hand, and I accepted. The sweet-tempered young woman who adored you does not exist anymore, and I'm sorry I'm not as naïve as I used to be. I suppose that means I cannot be used or manipulated anymore."

A muscle worked in his jaw, and he watched her. She wondered what was going through that clever mind of his. He finished his tea and placed his cup down on the small table before them. "I never manipulated you. That is unfair, Paris."

"Well, life is unfair, and so too are sexual encounters some of the time. I'm sorry you did not get to spend last evening, but I'm certain you could have handled that well enough on your own later. No harm done."

"No harm done?" he repeated. "It took me half an hour to get my cock to lower enough for me to leave the Duncannon's music room."

His words conjured an image in her mind, and she chuckled. "I'm terribly sorry. How painful that must have been." She paused. "But you will be happy to know that I enjoyed myself most splendidly, and I'm looking forward to the next time you please me."

"Really?" he drawled. "Please you? Is there no room for me to have enjoyment also? You know that I want you still."

"I know," she said. "And we will not always be at balls and parties where time is of the essence."

"Like we are now?" he queried, glancing at the closed door. "Can we not enjoy each other's company somewhat now? There is no one to interrupt us."

Paris took in his long legs, how he sat in the chair and yet seemed to take up all the space in the room. So commanding and authoritative, and yet last night, he had been pudding in her hands. Hers to do with as she pleased, and she was pleased very much.

"What do you have in mind?" she heard herself ask, wondering if she would ever be able to deny him anything, and doubting that thought immediately.

. . .

Dominic rubbed a hand across his jaw as he debated what to do with the little minx who sat across from him. The determined challenge in her blue eyes sparked his own, and all kinds of wicked and willful ideas floated before him.

One front and foremost—he wanted to kiss her. To press his lips against those sinful ones of hers and make her succumb to him. Give her heart to him once more.

But stubborn his Paris had always been, and it was one trait she had not lost in the five years they had been apart. He stood and came and sat beside her.

"I did think about taking myself in hand last night. In fact, whenever I thought of you, my cock hardened, and right along with that attribute, annoyance thrummed through every portion of my being."

She grinned, seemingly pleased at his words.

He shook his head. "I do not think this is something to be proud of, Paris. My balls were blue all evening, and I think it is only fair that we make an agreement that we both find fulfillment whenever we have a rendezvous."

"Like now, you would like for us to be intimate?" she asked him before cringing. "I do not think I have time. I have an appointment with the modiste."

"Are you trying to torture me?" he blurted, starting to wonder if that was indeed what she was trying to do.

"Of course not," she said, her tone one of innocence, but he did not buy it. She was enjoying herself immensely. "I would never be so cruel."

"I'm not certain I believe that." Without warning, he wrenched her onto his lap, her hip fitting snugly against his cock. She wiggled in his hold, gaining a more comfortable seat, but did not try to escape.

One small win, he supposed.

She met his eyes and grinned. "What are you going to do to me now?"

He did not reply, merely slid his hand down her leg, clawing at her gown to fist in his hand. He slid it up her body, reminiscent of what he had done with her tunic last evening.

"Put your hand on my cock, Paris. We're going to come together this afternoon," he stated.

Her eyes widened, but after a moment, her tentative touch pressed against his chest, sliding down his shirt and waistcoat before stopping at the top of his breeches.

"Open the falls and take me in hand. I want you to touch me," he said, hoping he did not sound like a desperate beggar. For all his commands, authority, and the liberties he was taking, he certainly felt like one.

TWELVE

P aris fought not to get pulled into the sweet seduction that Dominic always evoked in her. It had always been like that between them from the first moment they met.

A spark that, no matter how much he may have fought against it, still burned bright and hot. Even now, after all that had passed between them, it was there, simmering, pulling them closer, no matter how much Paris wished it did not.

His hand slid against her mons and heat thrummed through her. She let him touch her, stroke her aching flesh, and tease her to a fevered pitch.

So delicious. So hot and what she had craved for so long. She had always enjoyed sleeping with her husband, he had been handsome and kind, and there was nothing not to enjoy.

But no matter the toxic, cruel past she shared with the man in her arms, having Dominic touch her had always been like a firestorm of desire and need that would not recede.

"Touch me, please, Paris. I beg of you." His voice sounded hoarse, torn, and she could not deny him.

She reached for him, flicking open his falls. His cock sprang into her hand, and she wrapped her fingers about it, stroked him to his base, and teased the hardened member.

He was so soft and yet hard as stone beneath her palm. She glanced between them, and the sight of them giving each other pleasure was more than she could bear.

"Dominic," she moaned.

He clasped her cheek in his hand and pulled her near. "Kiss me, Paris. Please," he begged.

She shook her head, knowing that if she gave in to that one demand, there would be no turning back. She would not be able to deny him anything and would once again be that pitiful, sad young woman she had been when she first came to London. A woman with nothing who had somehow fallen in love with a viscount, only to have all her hopes and dreams crushed.

No, she would not give him that power over her again.

She tightened her hold on his manhood, increasing her pace. His cock hardened further, the head of his erection purple and oozing with his seed.

A magnificent sight to behold.

He slipped a finger into her, and she gasped, having not expected such exquisite torture. She undulated on his hand, riding him, wanting him. Heat and moisture pooled at her core, but she did not care. She would take all she could from him, make him need her, unable to live without her, before he, too, learned what it was like to lose everything for no reason whatsoever.

No worthy reason, in any case.

"Yes, Dominic," she moaned as spasm after delectable spasm shot through her body. She clutched at him as her orgasm ripped along every nerve in her body, tremor after tremor that left her spent.

"You're so beautiful," he whispered, stealing a kiss against her neck. He stayed there, bestowing small nibbles on her ear that made her shiver.

Paris turned her attention to his cock, willing to let him have this one pleasurable moment. She unhooked his waistcoat and pushed up his shirt.

She slipped off his lap and kneeled before him. His eyes widened, and desire burned bright and hot in his brown eyes.

"What are you doing, Paris?" he asked, a slight tremor in his tone.

"Making you come," she explained, taking him in hand and stroking his cock. He was a large man, and she remembered their one night together.

After her initial discomfort, his consideration, his need to make her enjoy herself had left her breathless, aching with hunger. He had not disappointed her, bringing her to an orgasm that had enlightened her.

To this day, she regretted what had happened between them. An opportunity lost for sure. They would have done well together. She had always thought so because deep down, she believed, no matter what he had said to her in the Romney library, that he had loved her. That he had been persuaded away from her was the only reason he had cut her from his life.

His manhood strained, the veins pulsing as she teased him, stroked, and played.

"Suck me," he begged, his hands clasping the cushions on the settee with a tenacious grip.

She shook her head, not willing to go that far. Not today, at least, but in time maybe she would. "Be patient, my lord," she teased, increasing her strokes to a steady pace. "We have only just begun."

He growled, watching her, his eyes heavy with need. His heady gaze made her stomach flutter. She had not seen him look at her like that, hungry and determined for some time.

A small, ridiculous part of her liked it. Wanted him to be the sweet, courteous man he once had been. While another would take all of these looks and feelings she evoked and throw them back at his face.

Just as he had done to her.

"Yes, damn it, Paris." His cock strained more in her hand, and she felt his manhood pulsing as he spent over his chest, the pearl-colored liquid spilling against him.

She sat before him, watching as he caught his breath. He reached for her, touching her cheek and meeting her eyes.

"Thank you," he breathed. "But you know it only makes me want you more," he admitted, leaning forward. "Give yourself to me, Paris. We can be as we once were. Forgive the wrongs and be happy."

If only they could, but the wrongs were too great. She wanted to rail at him that he had left her before even finding out if their one night together had resulted in a child.

How could he have done that to her? To this day, she could not fathom it.

She supposed it could have been his youth, his family pressing him to do better, but he was already the viscount. He could have chosen for himself and be damned what his family thought.

Paris pushed away from the settee and pulled the hand-kerchief from Dominic's waistcoat, dropping it onto his stomach. "You best clean yourself off and go before too much time has passed. I do not need my servants talking about the goings on in this room."

He clasped the handkerchief and did as she asked. Without another word, he pulled down his shirt, securing it in his breeches before buttoning up his waistcoat. "Will I see you at Lady Hirch's rout this evening?"

"Yes," she said, sitting beside the fire and thankful for the space between them. She would not succumb to his charm, nor his desperate words of reconciliation.

She could not be so weak as to fall for such sweet, meaningless words yet again.

"But you really ought to court a young woman who is seeking a husband, as you are a wife. I'm not that lady, Dominic. I will never be that lady again," she stated, trying to force him to see sense. To not look in her direction for something she would not give him.

He had his chance, and he had thrown her to the curb. She would not allow him to hold all the power ever again.

He chuckled, but she could hear the uncertainty in his tone. Hopefully, with any fortune, he was starting to understand what she would and would not give.

"I shall see you this evening," he said, bowing and walking from the room.

Paris sighed and slumped back onto the chair, thankful to be alone. If only to gain her equilibrium. She could not think straight when he was around and needed to be strong. Perhaps her plan to hurt him should stop, especially when she feared that he would not be the only one in pain at the end of their affair.

. . .

Dominic stood in the upstairs parlor of Lady Hirch's rout. The rooms were all a crush, people mingling, talking, drinking, and yet he felt as though no one was saying anything at all.

He spied Lord Lupton-Gage and made his way over to him, bowing over her ladyship's hand in greeting. "So good to see you both. With this crowd, it is hard to find anyone's acquaintances."

Lady Lupton-Gage chuckled and sidled up closer to her husband. "We are off to the Jenkin's rout after this one. Who would have thought so many people were in London at this time of year?" she said.

"Very true," Dominic agreed.

"How is your friendship with Lady Hervey? Have you settled matters with her?" Gage asked him.

Dominic glanced at her ladyship, and Gage waved his concerns aside. "Do not concern yourself with the marchioness. There is nothing that I keep from her," he said, his lips twitching in an attempt to hide his grin.

Dominic sighed and turned to watch everyone else who walked the halls and rooms of the town house. "I do not know what is happening between us, in all honesty. I feel as though I'm at sixes and sevens. I have made my feelings known, and there are times where I feel as though she reciprocates those emotions, but then other times ..." He let his words trail off, fighting to find the right phrases to say aloud. Expressions that would not offend or give away too much of what they had done together.

"What happens at those other times?" Gage queried, the concern in his tone giving him the strength to speak what he feared deep within him.

"That she is there, but she is not, if that makes any

sense at all. I do not know what she wants, and sometimes I question if she even likes me, and then other times there is nothing that will keep us apart."

"Have you asked her?" Gage asked him.

"I have tried, and I have been honest. I have apologized for my treatment of her. I was young and a fool, listening to the wrong people, and I've admitted that to her, but I feel it's not enough. I feel she does not believe me and that I will not win her." He shrugged, frowning at his explanation. "I feel as if I have already lost her or that I never really had the chance of winning her at all."

"Being young is hardly an excuse, my lord," Lady Lupton-Gage quipped. "You broke her heart, and while I'm sorry for you, I must side with Lady Hervey on this. I do not think several days into the Season you could expect her to be compliant and do everything that you wish." She chuckled, but the sound was mocking. "A woman's heart does not heal so quickly, and I think you will need to grovel much more than you have already before you receive forgiveness in earnest." She leaned toward her husband and whispered something in his ear before she said, "If you'll excuse me. I see my friend Julia."

Dominic looked at Gage and noted his friend's thoughtful expression. "It seems the marchioness is angry with me also. I cannot win this Season. I'm doomed for failure."

Gage clapped him on the back, sighing. "Come, man, there is no need to be so melancholy. You must rally, remember your goal, which is?" he asked him.

"To earn Lady Hervey's trust and love once more. Have her be my wife before the Season ends."

"All possible when you set your mind to it," Gage said. He waved in the direction of his wife. "My heart does have a point, however. Do not expect forgiveness overnight. You may burn in the bedroom, but men can do that as well as women and have no emotional attachment. You must court her. Make her remember what fun and laughter you once shared. What you can share again if she is willing."

Dominic thought over his friend's words and realized he could not seduce her to his way of thinking. He had to make her fall in love with him again with traits that attracted her, to begin with. He frowned. If only he knew what they were ...

THIRTEEN

P aris accepted the note from her butler and broke the seal, skimming the missive. She stood and walked to the window and felt her mouth gape at the sight before her.

"He is waiting for you, my lady. What would you like for me to tell his lordship?" Frederick asked behind her.

For a moment, she watched Lord Astoridge tidy his hair as he sat in the black curricle, his matching gray horses docile as they waited. She sighed at the sight of him. He was so handsome, still made her heart beat fast, and yet behind that beautiful visage hid a man capable of cruelty. Of unfeeling words that were powerful enough to break the strongest of hearts.

He spoke to two ladies who passed her town house. She rolled her eyes at their tittering from his attention. Did every lady simper around the viscount? She had started to think they did.

"I will go and change. Tell his lordship I'll be out directly."

"Yes, my lady," she heard Frederick say before she walked from the room.

With the help of her maid, it did not take her long to change into her blue carriage dress with frogging along its hem and cuffs. Paris slipped on her bonnet and started downstairs, wondering where their little expedition would lead them today.

A footman opened the door, and she stood at the threshold, fighting the urge to sigh with delight as Lord Astoridge jumped down and came to collect her, his smile and bright eyes reminding her of times past. Much happier times when they had stolen away together without anyone's notice.

"Lady Hervey, your carriage awaits," he said, sweeping into a ridiculously low bow that was fit for a queen, not a countess.

"Lord Astoridge, how very surprising to see you here today. I thought you may have been far too tired after last night's routs. From what I heard, there were several."

His lips thinned into a displeased line, and he stepped closer, taking her hand and kissing it. His lips pressed softly against her gloves, and she felt the shock of his touch all the way to her toes.

"You mean the many routs I attended that you did not? I searched for you everywhere, and by the third at Lord Flowers, I realized that I had been played."

Paris couldn't help but laugh, having not known how fun it would be to trifle with him a little. And missing a few *tonnish* entertainments wasn't so very bad. "I do apologize, my lord. I had a megrim."

"Really?" he drawled, his tone one of disbelief. "But, never mind, we are together now, and I'm stealing you away to Richmond for a picnic."

The idea sounded charming, not that she would boast so much to him. "I hope you have packed a hearty meal for us both. The ride to Richmond is an hour at the least," she said.

He led her toward the carriage and helped her up before joining her and taking up the reins. The horses moved forward with a flick of his wrists, and they were soon steering out of the bustling streets of Mayfair.

"I have packed a fine fare and one you will enjoy, trust me," he said, smiling at her.

Paris couldn't help but grin back. A day out of London, no calls, and no need to make any in return did sound heavenly. In fact, last evening, after deciding to forgo the routs she had enjoyed a night in at home, she read more of her book and had an early night, instead of stumbling into her house at atrocious hours of the morning.

"That sounds divine," she said. They kept a steady pace, the roads growing quieter the farther they traveled out of town. Soon they were clipping along at a steady pace toward the park. This morning, there was no cloud in the sky or a dash of wind.

Every so often, they would travel under a copse of trees, and Paris glanced up and watched the dappled light as it played upon them both.

She caught Dominic watching her with a small, wistful smile and she inwardly sighed. For all her anger at him, her resentment, he was the one man who could make her want things no lady ought.

Well, perhaps they should, in truth. If women took and demanded more of the male species, maybe there wouldn't be so many prickly matrons about the *ton*.

"You should not look at me like that," she warned, needing to stop the uncomfortable feeling that rose within her whenever around Dominic. The sensation of falling under his charm like the nincompoop she once was. "You ought to save such looks for Lady Esme."

He shook his head, but his grin remained. "I've decided I want you, Lady Hervey, and I'm not afraid to admit what I want. Now," he paused, picking up one of her hands and kissing her palm, sending a riot of sensation through her that she did not need, "you may disagree with my plight and fight it at every turn, but I'm going to win your heart back, my lady. Even if it is the last thing I do on this fine earth."

"You are very sure of yourself," she said, a little part of her pleased that no matter how cutting she had been, he had not backed away. Was he in earnest? Did he truly mean what he said?

Maybe people could change in time, grow and learn.

There was no reason why Dominic could not. But possibly only if he kept away from his meddling mama.

"I do not think the dowager Astoridge would agree with you on your plight, my lord."

"My mama can concern herself with my sisters this Season and not me," he said, his tone harder than she had heard it all morning.

Not wanting to put a damper on their outing by talking of his mother, who loathed her, she rallied and looked ahead. "May I have a go steering the horses? I've never done so before."

"You have not?" he asked, surprise in his voice. "Of course."

Paris did not say a word when he reached behind her and wrapped her in his arms. His hands closed over hers and slipped the reins between her fingers.

"Now, firm but giving hold on the reins. There is no need to be harsh on the horse's mouths," he said.

She nodded, taking the reins, a little thrill of delight running through her at being in control of two large horses. They trotted along the graveled road, and she kept watch for oncoming carriages or twists and turns on their path.

"In time, you could control the horses with merely one hand, a little twist one way, a smidge the other, and they will turn accordingly."

Paris nodded, taking in all that he said. A carriage appeared before them, and he reached about her, guiding her hands but not taking control.

"Ease to one side of the road, now. There is plenty of room for both carriages to pass safely."

Paris did as he said and chuckled when the carriage moved past them, free and safe. "I did it," she gasped, smiling at him.

He smiled back, both of them closer than they ought to be. His arms were still about her, and for a moment, she forgot where they were and what they were doing.

One of the horses snickered, and she jumped, turning back to watch where they headed and thankful that they had not come upon a corner she had not been ready for.

The last thing she wished to do was end up in a ditch on the side of the road. That would never do.

Dominic sat away from her, relaxed on the carriage seat. "You are already proficient, my lady," he said.

She shook her head, enjoying their banter but knowing he was not in earnest. "Why, I thank you for the compliment. I do not think I could do this for long. My arms are already aching."

He chuckled and reached across, taking the reins, which she was more than happy to relinquish. "You will soon get used to the horse's pull with time and more practice. That is why you ought to leave a little room for movement from the animal. If you remember my advice, you will not end up with pulled muscles across your shoulders and neck."

"I shall retain it," she said, holding her hands in her lap, content to enjoy their ride out into the country. "You have not told me of your sisters, who I understand are in town this Season. Are they enjoying the many balls and parties? Have they been to Almacks yet?" she asked him.

He groaned, rolling his eyes. "I'm to take them there on Wednesday evening." He glanced at her. "You would not care to attend also? My mother cannot make it, another event she cannot possibly miss, or so I'm told, and I could use the help. I'm certain they would love to meet you."

Paris hesitated to reply, unsure she wished to return to Almacks, but the desperation on his visage broke through her refusal, and she agreed. "I can help you, my lord. I look forward to meeting them both."

His smile made her heart beat fast. "They are looking forward to meeting you too."

CHAPTER
FOURTEEN

S o far, Dominic's plan was working perfectly well. Today would have a pleasant outing, a picnic and good conversation, and nothing more. He would not push Paris to be intimate with him nor insinuate that he wished to strip her of her pretty carriage dress and have his way with her on the grass. Nothing.

The pleasure of her company was all he required, and he hoped that today was the start of a new friendship between them.

A renewed beginning that they deserved.

He caught sight of her glancing up through the trees as they passed beneath them, the dappled light playing across her pretty features. She made his breath catch, and he cursed himself a fool for letting her go.

He could only thank God for small mercy's that he had not known she married. He could not have stomached such a truth.

But soon, she would be his again. She would see that he adored her and wanted only her and no one else in the *ton*.

He just hoped she would not find out how deficient his finances were before she fell at his feet.

She would not have him then. She would think he had been a liar, a cad who played her a second time to gain the money she inherited.

Not that he knew for sure that she was a wealthy widow, but there had been talk that Lord Hervey left her a sizable sum to keep her well for the remainder of her life.

"My sisters Lady Anwen and Lady Kate are twins, if you do not recall. At eighteen, you can understand that they're both very opinionated, and those opinions usually mean that everyone else is wrong and they are right." He laughed. "But in all honestly, they are the best of friends, and I adore them. I hope they both find love."

Paris sighed at his side, staring ahead as if lost to her own world. For a moment, he thought she might not have been listening. "You sound as if you've become a romantic, my lord. Do not say it is so," she teased.

"There is no shame in being a romantic. Why even now, I cannot believe how fortuitous I am to be here with you, have your company once again. I have missed you," he admitted.

She rolled her eyes, but a pretty pink blush stole across her cheeks. "You always had a way with words."

"I only have a way with words when what I say is true." They came to a corner, and he slowed the carriage, turning with little trouble.

"This place we're to picnic. Have you been here before?" she asked.

"Several times. Sometimes during the heat of summer, when we were in town for the Season, we would come up here to swim. This property abuts Richmond Park, but is on private land."

"Oh, there's a river? How wonderful. I shall like to dip my toes."

He glanced at the sky, the sun getting higher each minute. "Well, it is certainly warm enough for such enjoyment today," he said.

They traveled for several more minutes before he pulled the horses beneath a copse of large trees that offered ample shade. He watched as Paris moved toward the river while he unhitched the horses and tied them to nearby trees before grabbing the picnic basket and joining her.

"What a delightful place. However did you find it?" she asked him.

"This land is owned by an acquaintance of mine, the Duke of Renford. I sent a missive to him yesterday telling him I would be here today. He does not mind so long as he's told," he explained. Not that he had told Renford that he was bringing Paris here, but even if he had, he was sure his friend would not have minded.

They set the picnic rug and basket under a small tree beside the river. The tinkling of the water was a nice escape from the bustling traffic of London during the height of the Season.

"And you swam here during your school years, you said?" she asked him.

He nodded, opening the picnic basket and taking out a bottle of lemonade his cook had packaged. He watched Paris, knowing that everything he had brought for them today was her favorite from when he had courted her five years before.

Her smile of delight warmed his soul, and he passed her a glass, relishing her taking a sizable sip.

"This is delicious, Dominic." She took another sip and

sighed. "Your cook made this, did she not? She is the only one who makes lemonade taste like springtime."

"I will tell her you offer her compliments," he said.

She glanced into the basket, her eyes widening at what she saw there. "Little cheesecakes, oh my, just divine." Paris picked one up and plopped it in her mouth. She closed her eyes, savoring the taste.

Dominic joined her, wanting to give her all he could, even if today's fare had cost him more than he had to spare. He pushed the dampening thought aside of his dwindling funds and instead focused on making their day marvelous.

"I will have to call on you and speak to your cook. Mine is not the best with French pastries, but yours always seemed to master them perfectly, no matter that she is more English than either of us."

"That is very true." He pulled out some summertime fruits and placed them on a plate to share. "Thank you for coming with me today, Paris. I know I wronged you, and you are not obligated to give me any portion of your time."

She watched him, and he hated the shadow that passed over her pretty features whenever he brought up the past. But he needed her to know that he had changed. That he was not the same youthful fool he had been.

"I've never been in a curricle before. How could I pass up such an opportunity?" she teased, picking up another cheesecake and slipping it between her lips.

Dominic forced down the desire that rose at the sight of her merely doing anything near him. "You are very generous," he said.

"I was happy with Lord Hervey, Dominic," she said. She'd used his given name several times today. The knowledge gave him hope.

"He saved me, and I will forever be grateful to him and the love he gave my children."

Dominic rubbed his jaw, hating that another was intimate with the woman he had coveted, the one woman he had adored above all else, no matter her common, simple heritage.

If anything, the fact she was not part of the aristocracy had only increased his like of her.

Or perhaps more ...

P aris knew she should stop eating the cheesecakes, but then, she did not want to insult Dominic's cook, whom she had always coveted for herself, even when he was in France.

The idea of stealing the Lady Astoridge's cook from her had been a temptation that, at times, was hard to deny.

"I'm glad you were happy."

She threw him a small smile. His kindness, his sweet nature that seemed so at odds with the young man who had courted her years ago, was hard to reconcile.

Hard to remain angry and bitter toward him when he seemed to want to change or at least repair the damage his abandoning her had caused.

"You should know that even if I forgive you for what you did to me, I do not wish to marry again," she stated, the idea not as solidified in her mind as it was at the beginning of the Season. Or even several nights ago.

Why she could not fathom. Maybe it was that the idea of taking a lover had reminded her of all she had lost with Hervey's passing. Or perhaps it was because the first man she had ever loved was sitting beside her, attempting to make her fall in love with him again, being sweet, kind, and saying everything a woman who had suffered a broken heart wanted to hear.

"This is a problem," he said, biting into a cheesecake and dropping several crumbs onto his coat in the process. "Because I'm determined to marry, and the only woman I wish to be my wife is sitting beside me. A woman who is being very determined to remain a widow for the rest of her days, even though she is too young to be placed on the shelf."

Paris fought not to grin. On the shelf, indeed. "Just because I do not wish to marry does not mean I will be sidelined in such a way. I agreed to help you at Almacks, and I attend many balls and parties and have friends in high places, do I not? It is lucky for your sisters that I'm good friends with Lady Sefton, a patroness of Almacks. Being so will help smooth their way through the evening."

"I could kiss you for being so generous," he said. "But I will refrain because I'm a gentleman."

Paris slipped another cheesecake into her mouth. Better that than kissing him herself merely because she was starting to think she was far from a lady.

CHAPTER
FIFTEEN

Paris could not remember a lovelier day out of London. Not that they were too far away. The sun shone, there was barely a breeze, and the water was not so cold that her feet, once she had removed her boots and stockings, turned into little blue ice blocks.

Dominic, too, was being the perfect host. He poured her lemonades and even went so far as to chill the bottle in the river when they explored. The horses slept under the trees, which was reminiscent of the times they spent together before everything went so wrong.

As much as she had once wished for Dominic to be her husband, she could no longer afford such luxury. The thought of him seeing her daughter, their daughter, sent a chill down her spine.

The moment he viewed Maya, he would know. He would see that she was his. Thankfully Lord Hervey and Dominic shared similar coloring. Both their hair had been of a darker shade, and their eyes brown.

But he would tell. She knew to the center of her being that he would see the sweep of her eyes, the twist of her lips that was the same as his when he teased. He would see, and then her daughter would be ruined.

"What are your plans after the Season?" she asked him as they walked along the shallower part of the river, the smooth round rocks beneath her feet not unpleasant.

I will return to Surrey and tend to the estate. I'm hoping Anwen and Kate are married and happily settled, but it is only early in the Season, and no gentleman has yet to show interest."

"And your mother? Will she remain in town or return with you to Surrey?" Not that Paris would wish the dour Dowager Viscountess Astoridge on anyone, and indeed not on Dominic's new bride, but her ladyship, when it came to her son, never seemed far away.

"The dowager house has recently been remodeled," he said, his face one of displeasure that Paris wondered about. "She is to move there before the year is out."

"You do not wish her to leave your estate?" she asked.

He frowned and caught her eye. "Why would you ask such a thing?"

She shrugged, staring back over the water. "You looked pained by the fact that she is moving."

"Ah," he murmured. "No, it is not that. There are other things at play that need attending at home. Mother is merely one of them." They waded for a few more minutes in silence before he said, "And what of you? Are you returning to Landon Hall? I understand the earl's estate is quite grand."

"It is substantial, but thankfully I have an excellent steward who runs things while I'm away, and I see weekly reports. I want my son to inherit a profitable estate, and I shall do everything to protect that legacy."

"You are better than some," he said, his words tinged with regret.

Paris studied him, wondering why he suddenly seemed so melancholy. Perhaps it was the talk of her children or her married life with Lord Hervey.

"But your sisters will be a success, I'm sure, and I look forward to meeting them. What time would you like for me to meet you at Almacks?" she asked, thinking it best to change the subject.

"Would nine be suitable? I know they are eager to attend at least once this Season, and they will be thrilled to have a countess who is friends with one patroness as their chaperone."

"It would be my pleasure," she said, meaning every word. No matter what had occurred between herself and Lord Astoridge, his sisters had nothing to do with it, and she would help anyone if she could, no matter their station or wealth. Not that the two young ladies needed to worry about the latter. Dominic was one of the wealthiest viscounts in England. There was little to concern them at all.

He came toward her, his breeches rolled up to above his knees. He looked so carefree and disheveled, and Paris had to admit that she liked him this way above any other. There was a calm to him here in these environments. Neither of them had to worry about what they said or how they looked. Similar to how she grew up at Grafton, a young country miss without a care in the world.

"You are the best of people, Paris. That you are even here, spending time with me, allowing me the opportunity to try to right the wrong I did, tells me of your forgiving heart."

Paris tried to laugh off his words but failed. She met his

eyes, and not for her life could she look away. He watched her, sincerity in every feature of his handsome face.

Do not fall, Paris. Do not fail yourself again.

But she could already feel herself tumbling. How could she not? Dominic was the first man she had ever loved. The one man who made her forget all reasonable thought and just simply ... need.

There was no logic to it. She ought to hate him forever. And by all that is sacred on the earth, she had tried, but she could not hold on to that hate perpetually.

She doubted anyone could without making them bitter and cold, heartless even.

She did not want to be like that, and while she wanted to punish him and make him regret his choice, she also knew, at some point, she had to let go of what had occurred between them.

Maybe they were too young. He was too immature and under the guidance of his horrible mama. She, too, was to blame. She should never have been intimate with him, not without some security, which at the time she'd had none.

A foolish young woman's mistake that she had almost ruined herself with. Thank heavens for Hervey.

"Maybe we have both been fools and made equal mistakes, but I do not want to punish you forever. It is exhausting trying to remain mad at you when you're so very charming," she teased. "Not," she poked his chest with her finger, "that I want to remarry. I do not. It would be best if you still found a wife who is not me, but I think we can be friends. Friends with advantages."

He wiggled his brows, and she giggled. "I have been enjoying our advantages," he purred, clasping her hips.

"So have I," she said. "I would like to continue them if you're in agreement."

"Oh, I'm in agreement." And before Paris could stop Dominic, he dipped his head and stole a kiss. It was a brushing of lips, so soft, so quick that had she blinked, she would have missed it.

And yet, that was not true. Her body thrummed to life at his touch. Her heart kicked up a beat and her skin prickled with awareness. She wanted him to kiss her again, and maybe something in her features gave away her reflections because he lowered his head a second time and kissed her once more.

D ominic felt the kiss with Paris right down to his toes. When he lowered his head, he hadn't expected her to remain where she was. He thought she would push him away, make a lighthearted quip, reminding him of why she would not kiss him, but she had not.

And it left him reeling.

He deepened the kiss, tasting her for the first time in years. She was sweet, tasted of sunshine and summer, lemonade, and everything that was perfect in the world.

He wanted to wrap himself up in the feelings she evoked in him. A sense of rightness, regret, and hope all mixed into one.

Her hands slipped up his chest before running over his shoulders. He felt her lift herself in the water on tiptoes to deepen the embrace, and he was there for all of it.

He wanted her. All of her, forever and a day.

He kissed her, threw all that he felt for the woman in his arms into their first kiss. He needed her to know, to sense that he was in earnest.

That he cared for her still so very much.

Loved her ...

The thought rocked through him but did not frighten him. Somehow, deep down, he always knew he loved only her. No matter that he had abandoned and left her to defend herself after being intimate, still right now, this very moment, she offered a second chance.

Gave him what he was unsure he could provide another should the roles be reversed.

She was far superior than he ever could be, and how could one not love such a person?

Their tongues tangled, fought for dominance, and he reveled in her taste. Willing and all liquid heat in his arms. His body reeled, his axis tipped, and he was lost.

There would be no turning back from here.

Dominic scooped Paris into his arms and carried her from the river, kissing her the entire time he walked toward their picnic blanket.

She was all fire in his arms, demanding and taking all that he gave her, and he would give her everything if she would only let him.

He lay her down on the blanket, and she pulled him atop her, taking his lips in a kiss that sent his wits skyward.

"I want you," she gasped, reaching for his falls and ripping at the buttons.

He clasped her hand, stilling her. "I did not bring you here today for this. We do not have to do this, Paris," he said, meaning every word.

"I want to, Dominic," she answered, her hands less urgent on his breeches, but still as determined.

He gave up the last of his fight within him. Who was he to deny a lady, and especially this lady? The only one whom he cared about so much that, at times, it physically hurt.

That he had hurt her haunted him, and he wished he

could change the past, but he could damn well make the future for them so much better.

If he could win her heart once more. Change her mind about marrying him.

He inwardly cringed, wishing he was as affluent as he once was. He did not want her to think any of what he did was because he needed a rich wife. He could marry anyone in the *ton* who sought a title and not so much blunt, but he did not.

He did not want to be that man. He wanted to be a better man.

Paris's gentleman husband.

It did not take him long to shuffle up her carriage dress. His cock ached and strained, the thought of being with her again almost too much to stand.

She wrapped her legs about his hips, and he breathed deep, fighting the growing ache in his balls, wanting to make her come before he spent like a green lad with his first lover.

He thrust into her, and all was right in the world. "Paris," he moaned, kissing the sweet sigh that spilled from her lips. "I have wanted this for so long."

Her fingers clutched at his back, pulling him into her. He did what she wanted, needed to please her. Give her as much enjoyment and pleasure as he would receive from this wonderous day.

"You feel so good," she gasped.

He kissed her, deep and long, thrust into her, giving her what she wanted. She met his every stroke and dragged him forward to the pleasure that taunted them both. His balls tightened, and he fought not to spend. He needed her to come. He wanted to hear her scream his name.

She rocked against him, and he increased his pace, their

coming together frantic. The first tremors of her orgasm ripped through her, and she screamed, moaned his name, and rode him as best she could while he fucked her. His cock hardened, and he came, pumping his seed into her, wanting her to thicken with his child. He wanted a future with the woman who lost herself in his arms.

With Paris.

CHAPTER
SIXTEEN

L ater that evening, Paris lay in a bath and sipped a glass of wine she had poured before dismissing her maid for the night. Still, her body thrummed and ached from her joining with Dominic this afternoon.

Not since Dominic had returned to town had she ever acted so outrageously. The thought of what they did, and where, left her skin burning. He brought out a side of her she had thought long lost.

But there it was, the fire and mischief that only he ever seemed to wring from her.

Was he wrong for her? Most definitely. He had already broken her heart once, but he seemed different now. A changed man. A man who had learned from his mistake and wanted to make amends.

But to forgive him and allow him back into her life could only occur in town. He could never meet Maya, or her ruse would be over, and he would demand answers.

Not that he would like the replies she would give, for it did not paint him in a pleasing light. Paris stared at the fire as a light knock sounded on her door, and the muffled sound of Millie called from the other side.

"Come in," she replied and turned to watch her friend, dressed for this evening's ball, enter her room.

"Your butler said you're not attending the Lincoln's ball this evening, and now I can see why. I thought you may be ill or something and thought to come to check on you," Millie said, slumping down on her dressing table stool.

"No, nothing of the kind. I'm quite well, as you can see. My only illness is Lord Astoridge," she admitted to her friend.

Millie raised her brow, interest shining in her brown eyes. "Really? Has there been developments I need to be enlightened of?" she asked.

"Yes," Paris sighed, picking up her wine and taking a long sip. "I was intimate with him."

Millie's eyes widened, and she merely gaped at her for several seconds without a word of reply. "What?" she stammered.

Paris sighed. "I was intimate with him again," she repeated. "I made a beast with two backs. I mixed giblets with him. Would you like for me to continue explaining?"

Millie raised her brow, nonplussed. "But you weren't going to do that at all. What happened, pray?"

She wished she could say she did not know, but she did. "He kissed me, and I was lost, transported back to the young woman who loved him so hard, too hard for her own sanity. But he seems different now. I feel he is truly trying to make amends, but I do not think I wish to marry again. He can never meet Maya. You know how much she looks like him. He would see straight through my marriage to Hervey and would not be pleased that his daughter carries another man's name."

"And what did he expect you to do? You did what any woman in our situation would do if we found ourselves abandoned, thrown aside, and pregnant. You did what you had to do, there are not many options other than ruination, and no harm was done. Maya is not the heir. Little Oliver has the title, and he is of Hervey's blood. You did nothing wrong, Paris, and while I think it is wonderful that you can forgive, do be careful. If you do not wish to marry again, being intimate with a man is a risk."

"I know, and thankfully I also know what I can do to prevent such surprises as I had five years ago, but I cannot seem to say no to him. He merely has to look at me, and I'm lost. I forget all that I promised myself and fall into his arms like a besotted fool."

"You love him still."

Millie's statement sent a bolt of fear through her. She did not love him. She could not. Not after all that happened between them. All the years she remained angry at him. Not to mention there was no future. She could never tell him the truth about their child. That was unfair to both Maya and Dominic.

There was nothing that she could change about their past. Nor could she alter who was her daughter's father. "I've been angry with him for so long, how could you think I still care for him so deeply?"

"Because you would not have been with him, allowed such liberties again if you did not. You can still be angry at Lord Astoridge and still desire him, still yearn for what you lost. Maybe that is what is closer to the truth?" Millie said, standing.

"You have given me much to think upon," she said, watching as Millie walked toward her bedroom door.

"Thank you for coming to see me. I hope you have an enjoyable evening."

"I will see you tomorrow night," Millie said, slipping from her room quietly and leaving her alone. Paris sighed and slumped beneath the water. Her mind battled with what to do and think of Dominic. They had made a truce, and the passion, the undeniable need still burned between them as hot as ever, but was that enough?

So much had passed between them. So many wrongs, mostly done to her and her daughter, unknowingly as they were.

She supposed remaining his lover while they were in London could not hurt. It would help her pass the time more quickly before she returned home to the country.

But he could not be with her past that time. The secret she held could not be known or found out. She would not hurt her daughter in that way, nor Dominic.

She had to keep her distance once the Season ended. Hopefully, in time he would marry and forget about her and their past.

Paris sat up in the bath and hugged her knees, staring at the fire that warmed the room. Her situation would have been much simpler had she kept him away. Not set out to break his heart as he had hers. Now her heart was not playing by her set rules, and that was not what she had intended.

But just like when she was a foolish debutante, her heart was not listening. And look where that had placed her in the end.

Brokenhearted.

· · ·

Dominic leaned back in his chair at Brooks and ran a hand over his face. This afternoon had been both wonderful and frustrating. He wanted Paris to give her heart to him again. To trust in the fact that he was no longer that immature, persuaded boy he once was.

A man now, he could make his own decisions and wanted her to be beside him when he did.

He glanced around the opulent gentleman's club, knowing his time in places such as these were limited. Soon he would be unable to show his face in such locales, not when the truth of his debt was revealed.

He inwardly cringed, hating to even think about Paris finding out that he was deficient in funds. She would think his courting of her had an ulterior motive.

It did not. She was wealthy, yes, rumor had it that Lord Hervey had bestowed upon her a sizable sum, so as to assure she would not be beholden to her children when they came of age, but that was not why he wanted her back.

He closed his eyes and debated telling her the truth of his situation. Coming clean and explaining the mistakes he had made and how that did not impact his choice to win her love.

While any rich wife would do, he knew the moment he saw her again that had she been as poor as she had been five years before, he would have still courted her.

But how to convince her of this fact?

There was no way of doing so. The only way he could get her to agree to marry him was if she never knew the truth until it was too late.

The thought shamed him, and he reached for his brandy, downing it in one swallow.

"Easy, Astoridge. You'll tumble out of the doors instead of swagger," the Duke of Romney said, laughter in his voice.

Dominic glanced up at the pillar of society and the man who had married Paris's best friend. "Your Grace, I did not think Brooks was your normal haunt."

The duke glanced about the club and then sat across from him. The leather of his chair creaked at the intrusion. "It's not. I'm normally at Whites, but Renford is back in town and invited me, and he's a good friend, you understand."

The duke watched him for a moment before summoning a footman and ordering a beer. "You look as if the world's weight is on your shoulders. Care to lighten it?" he asked him.

Dominic rubbed the back of his neck, not sure he should say anything to the man who was no doubt fiercely loyal to Paris. But then, maybe he could give him some advice and insight.

"I've returned to town to marry, a necessity, you understand. I'm not getting any younger," he lied. "But Lady Hervey seems determined to remain a widow, and I'm unsure I can change her mind on that matter."

Romney took his beer and sipped. "Lady Hervey is an independent woman, had to become one after ... well, better to leave that situation behind," he said.

Dominic ground his teeth, knowing full well what he eluded to. He cleared his throat. "Yes, best to, I think," he agreed.

"She has a family, and there is no need for her to marry. Other than further financial security, what can you offer her that no one else can? If you're trying to win her back, and from watching you during the Season, I'm assuming you are, what can you give Lady Hervey that she will not find with anyone else?"

The word love reverberated about in his mind once again and would not relent.

Nor did it scare him. If anything, it warmed his soul and soothed the fear, the anxiety that he was falling further and deeper into debt the longer they were in town for the Season. His sisters were costing him a fortune and the Season was not yet at its height.

"The one thing I can offer her, I still do not think will be enough. No matter how much I may wish for it to be the case," he admitted. "Other factors will soon dissolve that one element I can give that I believe I share with Lady Hervey, no matter how much she may deny it on her side. But it is not sufficient. I know that it will not persuade her."

Romney sipped his beer, his gaze thoughtful. "Then you will have to convince Lady Hervey that you are in earnest and it is enough and that nothing else is worth losing what you share. While I do not know the particulars of your life, and nor do I think you treated my wife's best friend fairly or with respect five years ago, I also know that this is not my life. Lady Hervey must choose, so if you are in earnest, and you mean all that you say and will fight for her, do not let whatever trivial matter it is holding you back from saying how you feel and what you want."

Dominic listened and debated all that the duke said. All good advice and everything he had thought to do and yet had not due to fear of rejection and the unknown. "And what do I do if she denies all I offer her?" he asked Romney.

The duke chuckled. "Well, if she is anything like my wife, the duchess, she will make you work for her hand. But do not be deterred. Nothing is insurmountable if you are honest and mean what you say." The duke stood, throwing him a small smile. "I wish you well, Astoridge. I think if you grovel enough, you may win this war yet," he said, striding away.

Dominic thought on the duke's words, and hope and renewed determination blossomed within his advice. He would win her trust and heart yet. There was no other choice. Not for either of them.

CHAPTER

SEVENTEEN

aris took Dominic's arm as he led her to the side of the Almacks ballroom and where she was to meet Lady Anwen and Lady Kate Astoridge for the first time.

Not even when they had been courting during her coming out year had she met the viscount's younger siblings.

The two young ladies, now women, watched as she made her way over to them. Their eyes held the same mischievous light that Dominic's had at their age, and both were striking.

"Anwen, Kate," Dominic said. "Please let me introduce you to the Countess of Hervey. Countess, these are my sisters, Lady Anwen and Lady Kate Astoridge."

Paris dipped into a small curtsy and smiled as the girls did the same. "It is lovely to meet you both. Are you enjoying the Season so far?" she asked them.

They nodded, their smiles warm and welcoming. "Lovely to meet you too, Lady Hervey," Kate said. "We feel as though we have waited too long to make your acquaintance. Dominic speaks so highly of you."

The young woman's words made Paris smile, and she glanced at Dominic, only to find him watching her. He was so handsome, so changed from the man she remembered who broke her heart. Again her mind tormented her, debated and muddled through all that he made her feel and to no avail. She did not know what to do.

"You are very kind, but I hear you have been busy in London."

"We are enjoying ourselves greatly, my lady," Anwen said. "Our brother has been doing his best to ensure our success, and now that you are here this evening, we're certain we will not make a blunder here."

"We would hate to displease the patronesses," Kate said, grinning.

Paris chuckled, coming to stand beside them. "You will not displease anyone. Merely remember your manners and do not go off with any gentleman where we cannot see you, and all will go splendidly."

Dominic cleared his throat, catching Paris's eyes quickly. "Do you remember our first evening at Almacks, Paris?" he whispered against her ear, sending a shiver of delight down her spine.

Heat kissed her cheeks, and she wondered at his question. How could he think she would forget such an evening? The night he had stolen her away in this building, kissing her until her toes curled in her silk slippers.

Even now, the thought of such a kiss made her long to taste him again. To be alone, just the two of them.

"Oh, we see Lady Anna Bell. May we go and speak with her? She's all alone," Anwen said, turning to them both.

"Off you go and enjoy the night, and do not forget to fill your dance cards," Dominic advised before they all but ran across the room to their friend.

Paris smiled, remembering those carefree days of being a debutante. How the thought of possibility, of an unknown future, filled you with excitement and expectation. "Your sisters will be a success, my lord. Look, even now, several young men are making their way to their small group. I think you shall have a double wedding before the Season is finished."

"Oh, I do hope so," he said, a small frown between his brow as he watched his siblings. "They are good girls ... women, I suppose I ought to amend. I hope they make a love match and are settled and happy before too long."

Paris patted his arm near where her hand sat. The feel of his superfine coat caught her attention, and she inspected it. "Lord Astoridge, you have a small tear in the sleeve of your coat," she said.

"I do?" He glanced at the small tear with surprise. "I will have to have my valet look at it when I return home," he said, his mouth thinning into a displeased line.

Paris turned back to the multitude of guests. "I do believe it was at Almacks that we first met," she reminded him, wanting to return to the subject of their courtship. The sweet, memorable part of it, in any case.

His deep chuckle at her words, too, brought back so many memories. "Do you remember our third attendance here? Should we sneak away and see if the closet is still unlocked?"

The idea had merit, and Paris nodded without over-thinking the subject.

"Can you remember where it is?" he asked her.

Paris almost scoffed at the question. Remember where

the closet was, indeed. It was one location she could never forget, and being one of the sweetest memories she had of Dominic, she had never had reason to.

"I do. I shall meet you there directly."

Dominic felt her reply to the center of his very soul. His body thrummed with the need to be with her again. To kiss and touch her, to remind himself that she desired him as much as he did her.

He wanted more than to have her desire him in such a way. He wanted her to be his wife, and this was merely one more step in proving to her that he would not disappoint her this time. That there was a future for them if only she would take a leap of faith.

It did not take him long to find the closet that held so many ravishing memories for them both. That none of their friends knew of their courtship had been a wonderful, freeing truth.

He opened the closet and closed it, attempting to be as patient as possible. That he had exploited the fact their friends had not known of his interest in Paris and had used it to his advantage later on dimmed his excitement, but he thrust it away.

He was no longer that immature, reckless boy. He was a man now and one who knew what he wanted, who he had always wanted. Had he thought to marry someone else, he would have, but he could never find the words nor the right woman to suit the viscountess title.

There was a reason for that. As the handle turned and the door opened, that reason stood before him.

He wrenched her into the small, dark place and kissed her.

Hard.

Their tongues tangled and danced as he walked her back against a wall, pressing their bodies together. His ached for release. He wanted to lift her into his arms and have her wrap her delightfully lean legs about his waist while he pleasured them both.

Her hand reached between them, rubbing against his cock, and he moaned through their kiss. "Paris, you'll make me spend like a green lad in my silk breeches."

An article of clothing he could ill afford to ruin, no matter how satisfying that would be.

She giggled and pushed at his chest. He watched, transfixed, and felt his heart stop as she kissed her way down his chest through his shirt and waistcoat.

Her eyes met his when she knelt before him, and he read the wickedness in her gaze. He swallowed, bit his lip, and reached out to steady himself on the wall.

"I'll not let you ruin your silk breeches," she cooed, untying each button on his falls with excruciating slowness. He took a calming breath, wondering if she would do what he damn well hoped he was imagining.

She freed his cock, and it dropped onto her hand, hard and all but begging for her touch. He gasped when her tongue licked the little bead of come from his tip. She closed her eyes, wickedness on her features before she took him in hand and guided his prick into her hot, willing mouth.

She suckled him, and he gasped, watched her, fought not to spend, to pump his seed down her throat as he wanted.

She worked him, her hand in sync with her mouth, pulling, suckling, teasing his length with her tongue, her teeth with restraint.

"Fuck, Paris," he swore, rolling his hips.

She murmured her delight, a small smile on her lips before she took him into her mouth again, working him, teasing him. Never in his life had he ever burned for another with so much need.

His balls tightened, and he knew he was close. With a pop, she pulled off his cock, and he took the opportunity to wrench her to stand.

He turned her about and pressed her against the wall. "My turn," he whispered against her ear, reaching down to hoist up her gown.

She did not move to stop him, her ass pressing back against his cock.

"I know you want me to fuck you," he taunted her.

She nodded, her hands against the wall and where she rested her head. "I'm glad you're aware," she said, throwing him into a spin.

He felt her ass, naked to his touch, and pushed her legs apart with his foot. "I'm going to make you come so hard, Paris," he said.

She hummed her agreement as he positioned himself behind her and thrust into her hot, tight cunny.

He took her with relentless strokes and used his hand to tease her little pebbled nubbin. She was wet, undulating against him, taking all that he gave her, and lights blazed behind his eyes.

So damn good. So fucking hot.

"I cannot get enough of you," he admitted, his balls tightening a second time. She reached behind her, clasping him about the neck, holding him close, and he felt her trembling.

Her orgasm ripped through her, and he followed. He

pumped his seed into her, and let her contractions pull his own pleasure forth.

He moaned, gasped her name, and took her until there was nothing left to give, nothing left behind.

But satisfaction.

EIGHTEEN

Paris sat in the carriage as they made their way to the second ball for this evening. Almacks had been a success for Lady Anwen and Lady Kate, and both women had danced multiple times.

Paris's body still thrummed with the pleasure Dominic had wrought in her. He sat across from her, and she could feel his eyes like a physical caress.

For several minutes she fought to keep her attention on the Mayfair streets, not entirely sure it was safe to look at him, but then desire got the better of her, and she glanced in his direction.

She should not have. His eyes burned with passion, with determination, and she could not look away, not even when Kate giggled at her side.

"Lady Hervey, I understand you have two children," Kate said, pulling her attention from Dominic.

Paris nodded, smiling at the mention of her children. "I do, yes. Lady Maya and Lord Oliver Hervey. They are at home at Landon Hall, but as per our tradition, they will spend the final two weeks of the Season in town with me before we close up the London town house," she said, wondering how she would keep Dominic from seeing her children. A situation she had not taken into account.

"Oh, how lovely. Our mama never let us go to town with her and Dominic when we were younger," Lady Anwen said, pouting at her brother as if it were his fault.

Dominic rolled his eyes. "You were bothersome," he explained. "And you know mother's disposition to children," he teased, grinning at Paris.

She chuckled, knowing how irritating his mother was to everyone else. But thankfully, she had not had the displeasure of seeing her again since her last interaction with the dowager viscountess. Although she had not broached the subject with Dominic, she could only assume her warning had been heeded, and he had told his mother to leave her alone.

"She will be at the Craig's ball, unfortunately, and will no doubt push us toward gentlemen that we've already stated we are not interested in."

Paris did not appreciate the sound of that at all. A Season in London ought to be fun and carefree, not filled with trepidation that you would be thrown before a gentleman who is old enough to be your grandfather.

Not that she knew that was what the dowager viscountess was up to, but she could imagine she was. She certainly wanted her son to marry well, and no doubt that went for her daughters also.

The idea of Dominic dancing with anyone but herself made her blood boil. She was so changed since she had first seen him again after all the hurt of their past.

But then, so too was he, which was fortunate. He was caring, had apologized for his treatment of her, even though he only knew half of what he did.

What would he think? How would he react should he know that she had borne his child? That little Lady Maya was his and not Lord Hervey's.

"Thank you for your assistance this evening, Lady Hervey, at Almacks. I'm certain Lady Sefton is now quite enamored of us," Anwen said, satisfaction twisting her lips.

Dominic shook his head and chuckled. "We will see soon enough, I suppose. Should you receive another invitation, then your summarization is correct."

"I hope Lord Devlin is present this evening. Or Mr. Kane for you, Anwen. They are the gentlemen we wish to see, are they not?" Kate asked her sister.

"Oh yes, Mr. Kane has a small estate in Reading and is worth a thousand pounds a year from what I'm told. Not a lot, I know, but he's deadly handsome, and I should think kisses very well."

Dominic cleared his throat and gave Paris a look of horror. "I'm not sure what you spend on gowns will be satisfied with a gentleman who is only worth a thousand pounds a year," he said, pulling at his cravat.

His words chilled a little of the amusement they were all having in the carriage, and the look of devastation on Kate's visage gave Paris pause. Was he putting someone's wealth above that of their heart's desire?

The carriage rolled to a halt, and the girls tumbled out before Paris and Dominic followed at a more sedate pace. "Why would you have said that to Lady Kate? So what if Mr. Kane is not as rich as you? She has a substantial dowry and can satisfy income more than enough for both of them."

"My apologies," he said, helping her with her cloak. "I merely meant I do not want my sisters jumping into a union merely because of a pretty face."

"As you did with me until you found out I was poor and jumped ship?" she bit back, not satisfied by his answer.

He pulled her to a stop before the ballroom doors, stepping close. She breathed in the deep scent of vanilla that drifted from his attire this evening and fought to keep her head. He smelled so good, but not good enough not to remain annoyed with him.

"No, nothing of the kind. You know what I did to you was a mistake and one that I'm paying for even now when you keep throwing it against me at any chance you have."

She walked ahead, knowing that was true, but what did he expect? Especially when he said odd things as he had to his sister in the carriage.

They entered the ballroom, and Paris watched as Dominic's sisters greeted their mother and were soon hurried toward a group of young ladies and gentlemen who stood talking some distance away.

His mother, once happy with her daughters' situation, turned. Paris inwardly swore when the dowager spotted her beside Dominic. Dominic's mother's mouth twisted into a displeased line as she sauntered toward them, nose high in the air as if she commanded the ballroom over the hosts.

What a snobbish prig she was, and how Paris loathed the woman who had been at the center of all her misfortune. Who had been cruel and unkind to a woman of no rank or fortune, and because of which her daughter now would never know her true father.

"Lady Hervey," she all but spat, taking in Paris's attire as if what she wore was offensive in some way. Beneath her exulted standards that were no standards at all. The woman's cruel and nasty character toward anyone she deemed unworthy made her so.

"Lady Astoridge. What a pleasure to see you again," she said, her tone mocking.

The dowager blinked slowly, and Paris fought not to smile. She hoped she understood that any dislike was wholly mutual.

"I hear that you helped escort my daughters to Almacks." She turned to Dominic, pinning him with a hard stare. "Why did you not ask me, my dear? I'm more than capable, and I've been in society much longer than Lady Hervey."

Dominic took two glasses of ratafia from a passing footman and handed one to Paris. "Lady Hervey was kind enough to accept my request of her, and there is no harm in others escorting Kate and Anwen. It does not always have to be us, and anyway," he said, taking a sip of the sweet drink. "Lady Hervey is friends with Lady Sefton, and I think it helped my sisters in their quest for a successful evening."

His words brooked no argument, and the dowager could not say much to what he said. Unless she wanted to look even more spiteful than she already did.

"Humph," she huffed. "Well, let us hope it does help them, for both need good matches. The Astoridges only marry well," she said, glancing at Paris as she said the words.

Paris fought not to glare at the old biddy. How could a person who had such sweet daughters be so vindictive and mean? It made little sense at all.

"My escorting your daughters will not hurt their chances of finding a good match, my lady." She paused, debating her next words and deciding to go forth with them. "Even a woman such as myself who started off with no fortune or rank when first coming to London had a successful Season. No matter the work that others put into my time here to try to make it not so."

The dowager gaped before narrowing her eyes. "I hope you are not insinuating anything, my dear. I would hate for us to have a falling out since you seem familiar with my son once again."

"Mother ..."

Paris touched Dominic's arm, halting his words. She had long learned to defend herself, and she certainly did not need a man to speak for her. She stepped close to the dowager so only she could hear. "I did not think we ever had a falling-in." Paris smiled, sipping her drink before pushing past the dowager, not caring that she knocked into her shoulder.

She made her way over to Millie, needing sane, kind conversation for several minutes. Dominic could deal with his mother. She no longer had time for her.

Nor would it seem the more time she spent in society that she could mind her manners, even to matrons of the *ton* such as Lady Astoridge. She could not respect anyone who did not respect her in return. Dominic's family or no.

NINETEEN

Dominic sighed as Paris turned up her nose at his mother and left them to speak to the Duchess of Romney.

He could not blame her. His mother was a termagant and a person that he, too, grew tired of when having to spend a prolonged period of time with. That he had lived abroad and should be happy to see her again had been short-lived. She was as opinionated and cutting as ever, and he feared she would never change.

Certainly not toward Paris.

"You cannot speak to Lady Hervey the way that you are. She is highly respected and liked in London. Not to mention that I like her also. You are only causing harm to myself and my sisters."

His mother scoffed at his words, her face pinched with dislike for the countess. "Like I need her, the little nobody, to help my family. We are wealthier and more powerful than the Hervey line. They may have the earldom, but our viscountcy goes back hundreds of years further than theirs, and we all know that the second earl only got his title because he was the king's second cousin."

Dominic sighed and debated telling his mother that the money was gone. That she ought to want people such as Lady Hervey's help in gaining her daughters a good match. Other than their sweet faces and characters, they had little to recommend them.

They both needed to marry rich men who did not care for a dowry. A rare man indeed in London society.

"I heard a rumor, and I must ask you of it," his mother said, watching him.

He had also heard the rumor and did not care for it. And he certainly did not want to speak to his mother regarding it. "What is the latest *on dit* you wish to speak of?" he asked anyway, hoping that it may be different.

"That you have romantic connotations toward Miss Smith?" she whispered, spitting Paris's name like it was mud in her mouth.

He ground his teeth, praying for patience. "I do not see how that is anyone's business but my own. It would help if you did not listen to gossip. It's beneath you."

"And yet you do not deny it." Her pinched mouth told him she was fighting to control her ire. The woman was easier to read than a book, and taking in the room, several guests had become interested in their conversation.

He shrugged. "I hate to tell you this, Mother, but I'm not a child. I may choose whom I see both on a friendly or romantic level."

She poked him in the chest, her nail poking his skin. "I will never accept her into the family, or her children. Do not travel that path again, Dominic. I will not care for it." His mother spied someone she knew, and her face burst into a wide smile, altering her visage from foe to friend in an instant. So changeable, such a bitter woman. He wondered, watching her move toward her friend, how she had come to be the way she was. He caught sight of his sisters and was glad that they had not grown into being like their parents, even with his absence. Their Season would have been a disaster then and a complete failure. No one wanted a virago, and certainly not one as a wife.

P aris stood at the doors to the Craig's town house and waited for her carriage to arrive. She had sent a missive via a footman to her home to send for her equipage.

The night had turned chill, and she huddled into her cloak as the sound of clipping horse's hooves on the cobbled road sounded nearby. Hopefully, it would be her carriage.

Thankfully the vehicle turned toward the house, and she prepared to return home. She needed her bed. The night had been tiring, pleasant, and equally maddening with Lord Astoridge's horrible mama in attendance.

A warm, large hand pressed against her hip before a deep baritone whispered in her ear, "Let me escort you home."

She glanced at Dominic as the carriage rocked to a halt before them, and a footman opened the door, letting down the steps. "Very well," she said, wanting to be alone with him, have him near her, comfort her after the trying night.

Taking hold of the footman's hand, she stepped into the carriage, and Dominic followed her. The footman closed the door, and they were soon ensconced in the darkened space.

"Drive around for a time," he yelled out, meeting her

eyes through the shadowed carriage, a wicked light burning in his.

She shivered at the thought of what he had in mind. She had never done anything in a carriage other than travel from one point to another, but something in his unscrupulous gaze told her he had other plans for them.

"I'm sorry about my mother. Again," he said.

She waved his concerns aside. Not wanting to speak of the woman anymore. She was a waste of one's breath, in Paris's opinion. "I do not want to talk of your mother," she said, the need growing within her, removing all thought of anything else but him.

His lips twitched before he quickly untied the carriage blinds, letting them drop shut, enclosing them further into darkness.

"What would you like to speak of?" he asked her, leaning back on the squabs.

He was so handsome, his chiseled jaw just begging to be held, his kissable lips to be taken in a searing embrace.

She bit her lip, wondering if she were bold enough to take more of what she wanted, just as she had earlier tonight.

She leaned forward and clasped the hem of her gown, pulling it above her knees. His eyes darkened, but before he could move she stood, going to him instead.

She straddled his lap, adjusting herself to press against the hardened mass in his breeches.

So fine, and all hers to do with as she pleased.

He gasped, clutched her bottom, and she pressed harder against him. "I could eat you alive," he murmured, closing the space between them and kissing her chin.

Shivers ran down her spine, and she tipped her head back, allowing him to do whatever he pleased, so long as she felt the sweet, delectable taste of ecstasy that he always seemed to provide.

She ran her hands down his chest, reveling in the feel of the muscles that flexed beneath her palms. It took little effort to free him from his breeches. His heavy, hardened cock slipped against her palm, and she teased him before guiding him into her.

He took her hard, thrusting into her, and their moans mingled in the small space.

"I want you. All of you," he said, taking her face in his hands and making her look at him. No matter their past, something in his tone, the look of adoration on his face, made her know with certainty that he meant what he said.

He wanted her to be his wife.

She had wanted to hurt him, to make him pay with his heart as he had made her pay with hers. But she could not do that now. How could she be so cruel when so much time and growth had happened for them both?

They were not the same as they once were, nor did they have to listen to others to guide them.

Paris did not know how to respond, how to tell him all that she had planned to ruin and crush his heart, and so instead, she threw herself into making love to him.

She rode him, enjoying the delicious slide as he filled and inflamed her body. His hands moved over her, guiding, caressing, teasing her to madness.

"How are we going to stop?" she asked, her body coiling into itself, the exquisite ache and taunting precipice that was just out of reach, but tantalizingly close.

"Why do we need to stop? We never have to stop. If only you would give me your heart once more. We could have a future, Paris. We could start a life together. I could help you raise your children, guide and love them as much as I love you," he admitted.

The first tremors of her orgasm ripped through her, and she clutched at him, kissed him as she rode him through her pleasure.

He did not follow her but waited for her to catch her breath and meet his eyes. "I mean what I say, Paris. I've never been more serious in my life, and I will spend every day of the rest of it proving to you that I mean what I say."

Paris did not know what to say or do. This was not what she had planned, but then, everything had become so muddled she no longer really knew what she wanted when it came to Dominic.

He loved her.

How was she ever to think clearly when she knew such a wonderful fact. It would have been much easier if he had not grown into the man he was today but remained the selfish, persuadable youth he had once been. It would have been much easier to walk away then, but now? Now she wasn't confident she could at all.

CHAPTER
TWENTY

T he following afternoon Lord and Lady Astor held an afternoon tea at their property that abutted the Thames. A yearly event that was either held through the day or as a nightly ball.

The afternoon was a little cool, with clouds marring the sky, and Paris wore a cream spencer over her afternoon gown of blue muslin.

The grounds were bustling with guests, everyone who was anyone in attendance. Paris studied the crowd as a prickling of awareness stole over her.

She turned toward the terrace steps leading into the house and spied Lord Astoridge. He stood alone, a glass of brandy in his hand and his attention solely on her.

A shiver ran down her spine. After their interlude in the carriage and what he had admitted to her there, everything had changed. The thought that he wanted a future with her, to be part of her life with her children, left her stomach in knots.

As much as she would have loved to be a family at one time, that was not so easy now. He would take one look at

Maya and know he was her father. The thought of telling him the truth after all these years left her fearful. He would be angry and hurt, confused, and would no doubt lash out at her concealing the truth. Maya herself, even if only five had grown up only knowing one father. To learn that Lord Hervey was not her papa would devastate her and impact her future. And although the past was not wholly her fault, perhaps she could have fought more at the time and demanded he take responsibility for the child that grew in her belly. Made him marry her no matter her lack of dowry. She had not.

Not that she believed she could have done so at the time. Not really. He had been arrogant and selfish then, and she had been terrified with fear. Had he found out about her child, she would have always had that hovering dread, just waiting to crash upon her life and ruin her and Maya for good.

No, she could not give him what he wanted, no matter that the more time she spent with him, the more it was something that she wanted also.

"Will you admit it to me now?" Millie asked her, passing her a glass of lemonade.

"Admit what?" she asked, taking a sip of the refreshing drink.

"That you are in love with Lord Astoridge." Her friend glanced in the direction of his lordship, who was now speaking to Lord Grose. "You know that if you continue this liaison, he will meet your children at some point."

Her friend's warning was heeded, and she inwardly cringed, having known that herself, a constant worry to debate. "I planned on hurting him. Of making him fall in love with me again, using him as I felt he used me."

"Which he did," Millie interjected, throwing her a pointed stare.

Paris sighed. "I know, but I can no longer continue with my plan. He has changed. He keeps apologizing and begging for forgiveness. He's loving, sweet, and mature, something he was not five years ago. I think he is in earnest, and I think no matter the risk, I should consider him."

Millie smiled at several ladies who walked by before taking her arm and leading her farther away from the gathered guests. "What did you plan to do?" she asked her.

"Hurt him," she admitted. "Like he hurt me, but I cannot do that now, but I also cannot ruin my daughter. If he finds out about her ..."

"It is his fault you were left to do what you had to, Paris. He is accountable for that. Whether he knew of the child or not is irrelevant. A child was always possible between two people when they're intimate and that he did not think of you but merely packed up his life and fled to France shows you how much he cared." Her friend paused, taking a breath. "Now, while I think you're right, and he's matured and changed, do not take the blame for this for one moment. He broke your heart and fled without a backward glance. He does not get to be insulted and hurt when the truth of his actions stands before him in the skin of Lady Maya."

Paris nodded, having needed to hear this truth from her friend, and she was right. No matter when or if Dominic met her children, he did not get to be insulted and angry at her. Especially when she had the right to be more so than him, she had been the one who had married another out of panic and necessity. And while that marriage had been a blessing, thankfully, it may not have been. It could have ended in disaster.

"You are right, of course, and I shall take each day as it comes. If he should so happen to meet the children, there is always a chance that he will not see himself in Maya at all. I could be worrying for nothing, and no one other than you and I know her real father."

"And that will not change unless you tell him the truth," Millie said, reaching out and taking her hand. "I shall always be there for you, Paris."

Paris smiled at her friend, glad of her support and lasting friendship. "And I you," she said and turned just as Lord Astoridge joined them.

"Your Grace, Lady Hervey," he said, pleasure in his eyes. His attention ran over her like a caress, and absently, she heard Millie excuse herself and leave them alone.

"I have missed you since last evening," he whispered, coming to stand at her side.

Heat stole down her back at the feel of his hand on her spine, one finger skating down the center of her back and making her skin prickle in awareness. "Really?" she asked.

"Yes, really," he agreed. The hunger and affection in his gaze made her heart stop and pleasure thrum through her. However was she to walk away from him? The idea of doing so became impossible to imagine, and she knew she could not.

So what to do now? Tell him the truth?

While that thought did not satisfy her, it may be their only way forward. She could not continue whatever it was that they had started and not be honest for the rest of her life.

The thought of starting that particular conversation made her blood run cold, and she debated when one told another of a child they did not know about.

How life would have been so much easier had he just stayed away.

D ominic had watched Paris and the Duchess of Romney for several minutes and could not help but think that their conversation was weighty.

Both women had appeared engrossed with their debate, and he had made his way over to Paris, certain that she was distressed.

"There is nothing wrong, is there?" he asked her. "I have not offended you in any way, I hope?" He hated the idea that she could think he was using her to slake his needs.

He was not. He was in earnest and wanted her as his wife, and he would not relent until he had proven that he loved her still. That he had never stopped.

"No, not at all," she answered, biting her lip as she watched the garden party guests mingle, talk, and laugh with each other. "But there is something that we need to discuss, and if you came to dinner tomorrow night, that would be best," she said.

"I would be honored," he answered, already looking forward to the time they would have alone. It would give him more opportunity to court her, make love to her, and convince her he was whom she loved and wanted as a husband.

Not that she had admitted such things, but he was a patient man, and there was no rush.

Except you have not been honest with her either …

The thought shamed him, and he knew he had to tell her the truth about his situation. Land on his sword as it were and hope that she did not throw him out as a fortune hunter, as he would seem.

"Brother, Lady Hervey, so happy to see you both. Mama has cornered Kate with Lord Cole's oldest son, and I could not abide his droll conversation, and then I saw you two over here and had to come to say good afternoon," Anwen said, smiling up at them both as if she had gained a most terrific prize.

"You should be supporting your sister," Dominic stated, looking for his mother and sibling.

"I thought Lady Kate mentioned being sweet on Mr. Kane. He is here also. I saw him over near the fountain speaking to Lady Astor," Paris stated.

"Mama will not let her speak to him. In fact, she dragged her away as if Mr. Kane was some dirty word not to be spoken. His fortune is not so great, you see, and Mama is determined we both make great matches. Not that I care, either way, so long as I have horses, I do not care a fig how much money my husband-to-be is worth."

"You may regret your decision when you're unable to afford one horse to ride," Dominic stated and regretted his words instantly when Paris glanced at him curiously.

"Money is not everything," Paris countered. "And your brother knows this. He is merely teasing. I'm sure if Mr. Kane came to call and asked for Lady Kate's hand, your brother would agree to the union. Would you not, Dominic?" Paris asked him.

He cleared his throat, nodding, yet the thought of his sister being poor and struggling left a sour taste in his mouth. He knew he should not, for indeed, he needed to tell Paris that, in truth, he was as poor as Mr. Kane and could offer little dowry for his sisters. Their happiness ought to be paramount to him, yet he did not want to see them struggle.

She would think his proposal to her, his attempt to win

her heart, was motivated by money. There was no way he could argue that it was not, for he could not change his circumstances. He had lost most of his fortune, only had his good name and entailed estates to show for it. Other than that, he had nothing.

Unless he married a rich woman.

"I shall speak to Mother and explain the situation and will ensure that Kate may choose as she pleases." Paris smiled up at him, and he grinned back, and yet his stomach churned at the thought of what he must do.

It was time he told his family the truth of their situation, and it was their choice who they married, even if those choices came with repercussions that they would have to live with for the rest of their lives.

In sickness and in health, for richer or poorer, just as the vows stated.

TWENTY-ONE

Dominic sat in his library and went through several piles of accounts that had come in just in the last week. Milliners, modistes, and hatmakers equaling hundreds of pounds.

He ran a hand through his hair, panic seizing him before he took a calming breath. How the hell was he going to pay for it all?

"Ah, here you are, Dominic. I have been meaning to speak to you," his mother said, gliding into the room as if nothing was awry. And why would it not be for her? She did not know the truth and carried on as if nothing had changed for the family.

But things were different, and they had changed, and he had to tell her the truth before another day passed. The expenditure for the Season was getting out of hand, and he could not pay what had come in, not by half.

"Please, take a seat," he asked, gesturing to the chair across the desk from him. "We need to discuss some important matters."

She threw him a confused glance before doing as he

stated, fussing about with the reticule in her hand. "I was about to take the girls to the modiste. There is a delightful riding gown in the window we saw yesterday, and I think it would go perfectly with Anwen's coloring."

"There will be no outing, and no more new gowns, gloves, shoes, hats, nothing."

Again his mother appeared puzzled and stared at him as if he had lost his mind. "Whatever do you mean? We are just halfway through the Season. The girls cannot be expected to wear the same attire over and over. That would never do."

"They will have to wear the same dresses, and they may even have to wear them next year also."

"I do not understand," his mother stated, her carefree tone of before replaced by one of trepidation. She ought to be fearful of what he was about to say, just as he was. The thought of saying something so heinous aloud was horrific.

"I do not know in any other way to tell you this, Mother, but there is no money. I lost it all while in France. Several disastrous investments put paid to the last of the money, and all we have left is our good name and entailed estates. These bills," he said, lifting several from the desk and dropping them from his fingers, "I cannot pay, and if you have not worn any of the new gowns delivered with these accounts, I suggest you return them posthaste."

His mother gaped at him and turned a deathly shade of gray. "You cannot be serious, Dominic. How could we have no money?" she said, laughing, but the gesture held no amusement. "We're one of the richest families in England."

"We *were* one of the richest families in England, but it would seem in my attempt to make us richer still, I failed and turned us into the opposite instead. I'm sorry to be so blunt, and I do not want to hurt you or my sisters, but you need to know the truth."

"But ... but how will we live? How will we survive?" Her voice broke before tears welled in her eyes.

"In several years, and if we're fortunate with good crop yields, we shall make up some of your money, but we shall have to let go of most of our staff. The gardens may suffer from fewer gardeners to tend your roses, and the girls will have to share a lady's maid along with you. We shall retire to the country and lease out this London home to recoup some money."

"Absolutely not." His mother stood and strode to the windows, looking out over the street. Her hands trembled at her sides, and shame washed through him that he had been so careless. "The girls are having their first Season. Who will marry them now once it's known that they have no dowry?" She turned to him, anger burning in her aged eyes. "I can only assume that you spent their inheritance along with your own?" she spat.

He had been such a prig, a selfish, disdainful lord. He could barely stand to think upon the boy he used to be. The one who used people and turned away without a backward glance. Paris was proof of that alone. But she was not his only sufferer. His family, too, would mourn from his carelessness.

"It is all gone, and the only reason I have not lost the estate and the London house is because I cannot sell it. We will all need to marry well."

"Is that why you're courting Miss Smith? Because you believe she has the money to save us?" his mother scoffed, glaring at him. "I do not care that her husband left her a dime. We do not want anything from her. The Viscounts of Astoridge only ever marry women of rank and fortune. Not a woman who married money and yielded from her husband's early death."

"You know that Paris and I have a past that goes back far further than her marriage or my losing our fortune."

"Look to Lady Esme. She's an heiress, has never been married, and is from a wonderful earldom. She will pull our family back to where it ought to be, and she is favorable toward you. I have watched her at several balls and parties and she's always following you about with her eyes. I think she would complement you well."

"I do not want a wife who complements me, Mother," he spat, unwilling to do what would make him unhappy. "I wish to marry for love. Why is that so hard for you to understand?" He wished she did not always have to see people for their monetary value instead of their inner worth. "I'm going to ask Lady Hervey to marry me, and I'm going to tell her that I come with nothing other than my title and two houses that are expensive to run. You need to accept this and stop your rudeness toward her. She is going to be your daughter-in-law, should she have me."

His mother laughed, a high-pitched sound filled with alarm. "Marry? Miss Smith?" she spat again. "Do not be absurd, Dominic. She is a nobody, a woman with no family or fortune, and from a small country town that no one cares to know. She lived outside the village in a cottage, for heaven's sake. Who has ever heard of the Astoridges marrying such lowly people? Had she not married Lord Hervey, she would have ended a governess or a lady's maid or some gentleman's whore."

"I will not have her spoken of in that manner," he yelled, standing and leaning over his desk, anger thrumming through him like a drum. " She is a good, honorable woman. Better than either of us, and you will respect her.

You will be kind and generous to her, for if she agrees to marry me, as poor as I am, you will owe your comfortable life to her."

"So you are marrying her just because she is rich, not for love at all?" his mother scoffed, shaking her head. "You foolish man. First, you lose all of the money our family relies on, and then you mock us further by marrying a woman who is wealthy, yes, but poor in every way that matters. My grandchildren will one day ask about their heritage, and what will she tell them, that she is a country girl from Grafton? That she was lucky enough to be friends with the Woodvilles, who sponsored her for a Season? Your children will be seen as less than what they should be because of the blood that runs through their veins. It is not enough that you make us insolvent, but then you mock us further with wanting to marry the cunning baggage."

Dominic prayed for patience before he said or did something he regretted. "If you cannot accept my choice as master of this household and as Viscount Astoridge, then you ought to make preparations to return to Surrey. You are not welcome here if you are going to be rude and uncouth. I will not have anything stop me from marrying Paris. I love her," he admitted, curious as to how easy that was to say aloud, even to his parent. "I need her to be the next Viscountess Astoridge because she should have always been Viscountess Astoridge. I believe that she loves me in return and will accept my proposal. I could not have her not accept me, for my life would hold no value if I were to lose her a second time."

His mother scoffed and strode to the door. "Oh please, Dominic. Are you a foolish burr who's crying over the past like a child? Do be serious and start thinking better than you are. She is not worth this family's time. She has never been, and you need to think of more than your pathetic heart or cock, which seems to be guiding you these days."

"Good afternoon, Mother. Shut the door on your way out, and do remember what I said. Reconcile with my choice or leave."

She threw him a smile that he had never seen before, giving him pause. "Oh, I'm not going anywhere. Good day to you, son," she said, walking from the room.

Dominic slumped back into his chair. Tonight he would ask Paris, and she would forgive him, believe him that his heart was true. He could not think any other way, no matter what his parent thought.

TWENTY-TWO

"The Dowager Viscountess Astoridge to see you, Lady Hervey."

Paris turned and looked past her butler to Lady Astoridge, who stood behind her servant, a bored and annoyed expression on her sour face at being held at the door's threshold rather than being allowed entry straightaway.

"Thank you," she said. "Please send her in." Paris stood and placed down the *La Belle Assemblée* she was flipping through on the settee before turning to greet the dowager.

Not that she believed her ladyship's visit to her today would be pleasant or end with them, friends. Her ladyship looked as if she were walking into war, and Paris schooled her features, not wanting the dowager to think she had any power over her, not in any way.

For she did not.

She was a countess now. A rich widow with an heir. Lady Astoridge could not touch her now.

"Thank you for allowing me to call," the dowager said,

walking about the room as if this were her own private parlor and not Paris's at all.

"Well, had I known you were going to call, I'm certain you would have known I would not have allowed you entry. But you're here now, so do sit down. I'm certain there is something that you wish to say to me, although I cannot imagine what. We have so very little in common."

The dowager chuckled, nodding at her words. "Oh yes, and you do use the correct term, Miss Smith, for you are common, no matter that you married Lord Hervey." The dowager came and sat on a settee, taking in the room further. "I remember this house from when the late earl's mother used to hold routs here. I see you have not redecorated, but then I suppose a woman from a small country village would not know much when it came to fashion."

Paris smiled, but in truth, she wanted to scratch the woman's cold and icy eyes out. How could someone loathe another merely because they had come from less than what she believed she ought?

"Are we to throw insults back and forth all day, my lady? Or is there something else you wish to discuss with me? We both know you're not here to make amends," she said, clasping her hands in her lap.

The dowager met her eyes and smirked. "Why, yes, there is something that I wish to discuss with you, Miss Smith. And I think you ought to listen to what I have to say before another word is spoken."

Paris sighed but nodded in agreement. Something in the tone of the woman's words made her stomach churn, and she had a dreadful sensation course through her as if something was wrong.

"I'm listening, my lady. You may begin," she advised.

Lady Astoridge collected herself and crossed her hands

in her lap. "I was informed today that my son is in love with you and intends to ask you to be the next Viscountess Astoridge."

Paris fought not to react to her ladyship's words. While she did not want to marry again and had told Dominic that multiple times, to hear that he had informed his mother, wanted to win her hand still, that he loved her soothed a little of the panic within her.

For all her denial of him, her anger, and the hurt she wanted to cause him, she could not deny that he had wiggled under her skin, and she loved him too. And while she had not admitted such a thing to him, she knew it was only a matter of time before she did. Before she allowed how she felt to run free and give him what he wanted. What they both wanted.

Marriage to each other.

"I'm certain hearing such a statement from his lordship filled you with pleasure, my lady," Paris taunted, not wanting the dowager to know how her admission made her feel. She had never been warm or offered the hand of friendship, and she deserved no insight into her heart now.

"My son's a foolish man, and that has been made even clearer to me from my discussion with him but hours ago. You will not marry him, Miss Smith, and it's because of what I'm about to tell you that you will not."

"Really?" Paris stated, raising her brows. "Do enlighten me as to why I cannot make this choice for myself." At this moment, she may even say yes to Dominic merely to spite his parent.

"Because my son has nothing to offer you. He has his title and estates, yes, but very little money to fund any of it. In fact, he has asked that I return to Surrey with his sisters and stop spending funds he has none of."

Paris swallowed the bile that rose in her throat, and she fought not to react. The glee in the dowager's cold eyes told her she had failed and had given something away as to how she felt. "What do you mean his lordship has no money exactly?" Paris asked for clarification. The thought of such truth was unbelievable.

"He made several terrible investments in France from what he explained and is now penniless, but for the small amount of funds we make from cropping and farming, of course. But that is not enough to keep us from having to downsize our staff and limit our living expenses. All very common and similar, I should think, to how you grew up in Grafton, but that is not how I shall allow my life to proceed. And so you see, he must marry Lady Esme, for even as poor as we are right at this time, I still will not allow my son to make us even poorer still by marrying a woman with no family, no people, no link to titles or connections. You will only bring us further down in rank, and I shall not allow such a travesty."

Paris cleared her throat, certain she was going to be sick. Was that why Dominic had courted her so relentlessly? Because she was a wealthy widow, separate from the fortune that had been left to her son and daughter? Did he need her money now?

Unable to sit a moment longer, she stood and walked to the mantel, leaning on the cold marble for support. "Why did Lord Astoridge return to England?" she asked, in truth not wanting to know the answer. Not really.

"He needed a rich wife and, with your past courtship, thought you would be an easier conquest than any other, and from what the rumors are about London, you have been too. He was not wrong in that. But I come here today to warn you of my son's plan. While I have my own reasons for not wanting him to marry you, I'm certain you also do not wish to be used. If you were to remarry, I'm certain, as any woman would want, you would like to have some modicum of affection in your union, not one built on lies and merely sought for what you bring to a marriage. Money," the dowager clarified.

Paris glanced up at the portrait of her and Lord Hervey and wished right at this moment that he was here with her again. To protect her from men who broke women's hearts and their mothers who wished to gorge on their pain.

"I thank you for being so honest with me, my lady. I shall not stoop to your level and tell anyone of your family's financial woes, but I will ask that you never call on me again. We have nothing to say to one another from this day forward, do you understand me?" she asked the dowager, having never loathed anyone as much as she loathed this woman right now. Not merely because she was cruel and took pleasure in her vicious manner, but because with her words, she also tore what little hope she had of a future with Dominic.

There would be no tomorrow now.

TWENTY-THREE

P aris sat at the dining table that was set for two for the evening and smiled across at Dominic. After his mother's call this afternoon, she had thought a great deal about how she would conduct the dinner they had planned.

The first course of stewed mushrooms was placed before them, and for several minutes she let the silence grow between them. If Dominic sensed something was erroneous, he did not say, and she could bide her time before she confronted him over what his mother had revealed.

The thought made her appetite wain, and she picked up her glass of wine, taking a fortifying sip.

"Thank you for inviting me this evening, Paris. I'm pleased that we're able to dine alone, just you and me. There is much I want to discuss with you."

She raised her brow. Did that mean he would bring up the notion of marriage to her without her prompting him first? For her agenda to work, she needed him to do exactly that, and then she could confront him over the truth as she knew it.

"Indeed?" she said, spooning a little mushroom into her mouth. Not that her appetite had been with her after the atrocious things the Dowager Viscountess Astoridge had said.

She watched Dominic, remembered back to his superfine coat that had a tear, his determination for his sisters to marry well. Even this evening, his suit was not the height of fashion. If Lady Astoridge said one thing accurately today, it was that Paris wasn't so up with the latest designs, but she could spot a suit well past its usefulness.

A little part of her hurt that he had fallen so low. But then another raged at the idea that he would only marry her now, offer such a sacred union merely because he had fallen so low. A way of saving himself from financial ruin when she had not been good enough when the opposite had been the case.

"You know how much I care for you, and I think these past weeks in London have been enjoyable," he said.

Paris nodded and turned to the footman, who stood waiting to serve them. "You may go. I shall call you if you're needed again," she said.

The young man left and had the smarts to shut the door behind him. Paris turned to Dominic and fought not to state what she thought of the enjoyable Season he was having with her. How he was a liar, and she did not want to hear any more of his untruths.

"Go on," she said, throwing him a small smile that hurt to form. She did not feel like smiling at all. In fact, she felt like glaring at the fiend.

He cleared his throat, adjusting his cravat. Was he nervous? She supposed he might be since he was going to ask for her hand. Not that he hadn't asked before, but tonight was different. His asking again and pursuing her felt as though her answer would either solidify or conclude their future.

How terrible his night was about to become, and he did not even know it.

"I know we've had a troubled past, and I hope these past weeks I have proven to you that you're the only woman that I want beside me for the remainder of our lives. I'm in love with you, Paris. I think back to that afternoon in the Romney library, and I do not recognize the young man who so callously threw what we had away. I was young and wrong, so unjust, and I hope you know that I shall never do such a heinous thing to you again. I shall never treat you with such little respect."

"Is that so," she said, slapping down her napkin and leaning back in her chair. "Then explain to me, Dominic, why your mother called on me this afternoon, warning me that you're going to offer me marriage to get your family out of financial strife?"

"What?" he stammered his face paling. "My mother called on you here?"

"She did," Paris stated, watching him, scrutinizing to see him squirm and try to get out of this dreadful bind. "She did not call with any genuine reason but one out of her dislike of me. She does not want me as a daughter-in-law. Miss Smith, you understand, is not exalted enough for the Astoridges, no matter how rich or titled I am now. But I digress. She came to tell me so that I would know the real reason behind your proposal when you asked for my hand."

He shifted in his chair, and she could see that he struggled to comprehend what was happening.

"My reason for wanting to marry you is because I love

you. It should not matter that I made some financial errors and now must figure some ways out of it. That has nothing to do with you and me, Paris," he declared.

She studied him, wondering if he believed what was coming out of his mouth. The man had no shame. "Your financial position has nothing to do with what is happening between us? Are you serious, Dominic? Because five years ago, it had everything to do with why you threw me over. After we had been intimate. After I had given my body to you. A privilege that I thought to be giving to my future husband, you. But that did not happen because I had no dowry. And now, you sit here, declaring that you love me while all the time what you really love is the money I would bring to the marriage. A way in which you could gain funds to see yourself out of bad investments.

"How dare you even ask me to marry you when all of what we have is a lie? You used me again, and foolishly I started to believe that you had changed. That you were truly sorry for what you did to me and our ..." Paris took a calming breath, having almost mentioned Maya in her anger with him. "What you did to me and our future I longed and dreamed of," she corrected. "I will not marry you, Dominic. I will not be your token out of debt."

Dominic did not know what to say or how to respond. Nor had he ever seen Paris so angry with him. But how to explain, to tell her that she was wrong? That he wanted to marry her out of affection and love, out of desperation for having to have her as his wife. Not a passing acquaintance or old lover.

He could not go another day seeing her dance and flirt

or being courted by anyone else in society. Should she remarry, it would kill him stone dead.

He loved her, but how to prove that to her?

She would never believe him now, and he had his mother to thank for that. And yet, the trembling of Paris's hands and the pinched mouth told him that perhaps even if she had heard from him and not his parent, she would still have acted the same. She would not have believed him, even if he had presented his situation first.

"I wanted to tell you. So many times, I wanted to discuss my predicament. I only told my mother of it this morning when several bills arrived that, even now, I'm unable to pay for. I had to inform her that I had lost the money I inherited and expenditures had to be trimmed."

"And then she ran to me to use that information to remove any hope I may have harbored for us." Paris shook her head. "I know I said I did not wish to marry, and up until you came back to London, I did not. But seeing you again, having you in my bed and in my life, even against my better judgment, I allowed my heart to open again for the possibility of us. What a fool I have been. You are a cad. A man who will go to any lengths, even pretend to love some-one, when all you really love is their money."

He shook his head, laying down the cutlery that he somehow still held in his hands. "That is not true. I wanted to tell you everything, but I was ashamed. I knew you would not believe me. I feared you would think as you now do. But it is not true, Paris. I do care. I do love you. I want you, not your money."

"You want me now that I'm rich, but you did not want me when I was poor. You are a liar, and whatever this vile, toxic thing is we're playing, is over. I will not be your mistress, your wife, nothing. I want nothing to do with you."

Dominic fought to breathe, his chest hurt, and for several horrifying moments, he thought he might cry. Gentlemen, viscounts did not cry, and yet the picture of Paris in his eyes blurred.

"How can I prove to you that I mean what I say? That I love you, truly love you so much that I cannot imagine my life without you in it," he declared, his voice high even to his own ears.

She stood, started for the door, and wrenched it open. "Please escort Lord Astoridge out," she ordered the footman. "Goodbye, my lord. I wish you all the very best with the remainder of your Season," she threw at him, the exact words he had uttered to her five years before in the Romney library.

TWENTY-FOUR

Paris returned to Landon Hall, the Hervey ancestral home, the following day and, over the past week, had indulged her children and spent every spare moment she could playing and spending time with them.

So much so that they now wished to return to their normal duties, leaving her to contemplate all that had happened in London with Dominic.

She stared down at the missive from him that had arrived with this morning's post, but she could not open it. There was little point in doing so. There would be only more professions of love, of all the reasons why she needed to believe him and forgive his actions.

Everything that she could not.

She would not.

He did not deserve a second chance. Or was it a third now, since he had been sneaky yet again during the Season?

The sound of her children's laughter grew louder the closer they came toward the library, and she slipped the missive into a drawer and smiled when they both came into view, their excited, sweet faces making her feel better.

"Mama," Oliver shouted, skidding to a stop before Maya had made the desk. "Joseph said we can go for a ride if you're in agreement," he said, both their little faces alight with excitement.

Paris reached out and smoothed Oliver's hair from his face before pulling Maya into her arms, kissing the top of her head. "Of course you can, so long as you do not go any faster than a trot and do not leave the lawns."

"We won't," Maya said, her voice high with excitement before they ran out of the room, leaving her as quickly as they came.

Paris listened to them as they shouted out to Joseph in the foyer before another voice caught her attention. She sat up in her chair, ice running down her spine.

"Good afternoon. I'm Lord Astoridge, and you must be Lord Hervey and Lady Maya," the man's voice said.

Her children mumbled something in return that Paris did not make out as she dashed from the library to stop the interaction. She paused at the threshold and watched with a terrifying slowness as Dominic studied Maya more so than Oliver.

His eyes narrowed, and he stood. "Tell me, how old are you, Lady Maya?" he asked.

"I'm five, Lord Astoridge. My brother Lord Oliver is only three," she said, pride in her voice at having been the elder sibling. Normally such a remark would have made Paris smile, but not today.

Dominic met her eye above the children's heads, and she knew to the very core of her soul that he had guessed. How could he not? They were identical but for their age difference.

"It is lovely to meet you both," he said, clearing his throat. "I would like to watch your horse ride one day. I see the stable hands are waiting outside for you both already."

"They are?" Oliver all but shouted. "Come on, Maya, we're wasting time."

The children rushed from the house, and Paris fought to school her features. There was a chance. Surely there was a slim possibility he had not guessed. Maybe he merely felt despondent that she already had a family, and he did not.

He strode into the library, pushing past her, and she knew the little bit of hope she had was futile.

He knew ...

Paris shut the door, hoping to keep the servants from learning her secret. "How dare you?" he said, rounding on her. "So high and mighty, to chastise me of my treatment of you, and all the while you have been hiding my daughter?"

Paris glared, fisted her hands at her sides, and fought not to scream at his audacity. "How dare I, you ask? How dare I sit in the Romney library after giving myself to you, thinking you are going to ask me to marry you and then having my heart broken when you threw me aside like some dirty, worthless wench you had tupped in the East End? How dare I find out weeks later that I was carrying your child and with no idea what to do to save myself? How dare I, you say. How dare you come here, say that to me, and think that is acceptable."

He crossed his arms over his chest, his mouth twisted in anger. "You should have told me. I would have changed my mind about not marrying you."

Paris scoffed, shaking her head. "And have you marry me because you had to? Have you marry me because of your duty? I did not want a marriage to the man I loved to be like that. I wanted you to marry me because you loved me. In a way, I'm glad that I did not tell you, for it enabled me to have a happy marriage. One without guilt, without my husband resenting me for trapping him into the union because of a child. I could not have borne seeing you start to hate me because of a choice we both made, and you would have. You were not ready for a wife. I should never have given myself to you. You were too young, and so was I. I made a foolish mistake, but I turned that error into a wonderful life for Maya and myself, and I will not have you come here and chastise me about it. You have no right."

"I have a right to be part of her life," he said, pointing toward the window.

Paris shook her head. "No, you do not. She has a father, and one she loved very much. You did not want to marry me, and not once did you ask me if a child resulted from our time together. You did not ask because you did not care to know. So do not act all hurt and put out now that you do. I will not stand for it, nor will I allow you to take from Maya what is rightfully hers. She is Lady Maya Hervey, and nothing will change that fact, not even your hurt pride."

D ominic stood before Paris, unable to believe what he was hearing. He was a father? How could he not have known? How could she have kept such a secret from him for so long?

How had you not asked five years ago if she was with child?

Disesteem washed through him that he had not. He should have asked, of course, that was a possibility whenever a man and woman slept together.

He had naively thought that it had not happened to them.

He slumped into the chair behind him and ran a hand

through his hair, unable to think straight. He was a father? But his daughter would never hold his name.

A problem that, in truth, was his fault. Had he offered for Paris's hand, none of this would have been a concern. And he could not blame her, not really, for the choices she made. For her hasty marriage to Hervey.

That alone ought to have sparked his interest, especially when he knew he had broken her heart.

"You cannot stay here. You must leave," she demanded, crossing her arms over her chest.

He nodded, knowing that was true enough. He had come here to beg for forgiveness, to ask yet again for her to give him another chance. But now? Now he was not sure he could give *her* one.

His mind could not comprehend that a little child who looked exactly like him walked but yards from where he sat. The twist of her lips and almond-shaped eyes were identical to his.

It had taken all of his good breeding not to gape at the child. She was a little mirror image. Any wonder Paris did not want a future with him. To have one would mean that he would have to have a relationship with her children, and upon first meeting them, he had been shocked by Maya's likeness to him.

At some point, Paris would have had to explain like he had to explain his lack of blunt. A point neither of them wanted to face, and certainly not own up to.

"You should have told me. I would have done right by you, no matter what you think of me and the actions of my past self. I would have married you had I known. I would never have allowed you to face such a trial by yourself."

"But you did. You did not even bother to ask me. That thought was not even in your mind. Admit it. When you left for France, all you cared about was rutting your way across the continent and forgetting about the girl you ruined at home. Do not try to blame me. Tell me what you would have done differently. Had you any honor, you would have acted like a gentleman, not some blasted, sinful rogue who pretended I did not exist."

"I never pretended you did not exist." He stood, striding to the door and wrenching it open. "I'm leaving, but this is far from over, Paris. There is much more to talk about, and when we are both less heated over all of this, we will speak. I shall see you back in London within the week," he demanded of her, slamming the door and regretting his bout of anger the instant he did it.

He strode past the butler and out the front door and, giving the children a small wave, jumped up on his horse and left. His life with Paris was far from over, and if she thought another year of his child's life would go by without him in it, she had another reality headed her way.

CHAPTER

TWENTY-FIVE

A week later, Paris found herself back in London, children in tow as she had promised them at the beginning of the Season. They had plans to go to Richmond and to go on a carriage ride about Hyde Park, but in truth, Paris had brought them to London merely because she wanted them with her.

Now that Dominic knew the truth of their past, there was little reason she ought to hide Maya from him. To do so would only cause talk, and she did not want anyone to think she was trying to hide her children from society. Even though having children in town was not the thing to do, she did not want anything to mar Maya's name.

She sat on the back terrace of her London town house and watched the children play hide and seek on the grass and gardens, their little squeals of delight and giggles pushing away the melancholy that had settled over her the past seven days.

Both she and Dominic had been wrong and had made missteps. Mistakes they both needed to own, accept, and move on from. There was nothing that could change the past. They had made errors, foolish, possibly wrong choices, but they were done now. Now she had to decide if she wished to hold on to the anger and hurt or let it dissipate into the past.

"You're back," Millie stated, coming through the terrace doors and slumping beside her on the chair. She waved to the children who smiled at the duchess before returning to their game.

"I am," Paris said, unsure she wanted to talk to anyone about what had happened, preferring to muddle and debate the whole situation again and again in her mind. Driving herself to distraction.

"Has Lord Astoridge called?" Millie asked her, leaning forward and pouring herself a glass of lemonade.

"No," Paris said, the thought of Dominic making her stomach churn. She swallowed, reaching forward for her own drink, wishing she would stop feeling so nauseated and nervous all the time.

Eventually, she could move forward again with her life, forgetting her dalliance with Dominic and everything they had said to each other.

Is that what you wish to do?

Paris could not answer her own question. He would not force her to allow him to be in Maya's life. He would not ruin his daughter in such a way. But did he not deserve to know her? Even if their daughter could never know the whole truth about his interest?

Paris glanced at Millie and noted her raised, curious brow. "Why do you ask?" she said.

"Well, he's been quite the curmudgeon, I must say, and glares at everyone when he thinks no one is watching. Which of course, I'm always watching because I know he's in love with you, and you are not in town. But now that you're back, I wondered if he had called."

Paris sighed, shaking her head. "No, he has not called, but he knows of Maya. And, in return, I know something of his situation that is equally shocking and ruinous, so I suppose we're even on that score."

Millie threw her a consoling look before her attention diverted to the children. "So you've both made mistakes, but it is clear that you care for each other. Even if, right at this moment, you're angry with him as he is with you, can you not forgive each other? As much as I dislike what he did to you, you love him. I know you will not be happy if he is not in your life, Paris," her friend said, reaching out and squeezing her hand.

Paris swallowed the lump in her throat, having a terrible suspicion that Millie was right. That she would not be happy unless she were with Dominic. They had made a mess of everything, but damn him to hell, she still loved him. Missed his stupid, roguish visage.

"I do not know what I should do or what I can say to repair things between us. There have been so many lies from us both. Each of us hiding things from the other, and I do not know how we can come back from that."

"You need to talk, that is all. I'm certain that if you go and see Lord Astoridge, he will see you and feel as despondent as you are."

Was Millie right? Would he see her if she called on him? There had been no word of him since he left her country estate a week earlier.

"I will watch the children and ensure the nanny takes them up for dinner if you're not home before then. Go, Paris. Talk to Dominic. If I'm any judge of character, he loves you, he may be hurt and as upset, but that is only because he cares as much as you do. Do not go another day without the man you love. I know you will never be content if you do."

Paris swiped at the wayward tears that slipped down her cheeks before reaching for her friend and hugging her quickly. "Thank you, Millie. For everything," she said before standing and slipping through the terrace doors. She needed to see Dominic and determine if there was a future for them. See if they could get past all the errors they had made.

She hoped they could.

Dominic lay on his bed with the curtains drawn. Today had been exceptionally warm, but a cooling breeze was billowing through the curtains in his room.

He leaned his head on his arm, staring up at the canopy of his bed, and thought of Paris. Always Paris. This past week he had done little else but rehash their argument, all that they had said to each other, everything they had hidden.

He had acted the bastard yet again. He had no right to be upset regarding Maya. Paris had little option and did what she had to do to survive. In truth, he was proud of her for saving his daughter's reputation from certain ruination, as well as her own.

"I do not care if he's resting, Malcolm. I'm going into his room. Now stand aside."

The sound of Paris's voice outside his door had him sitting up, his heart kicking up a beat. Her words to his butler worked, and she opened his door, closing it just as quickly and snicking the lock.

Seeing her again eased the pain in his chest and the sick

feeling that had plagued his stomach since he left Landon Hall.

Dominic sat on the side of the bed, watching her, wondering what she would say. He hoped it wasn't to recap their disagreements. He was certain he could not stand any more of that.

"What are you doing here?" he asked, not moving to take her in his arms, even though that is where he wanted her. With him, as his wife, his forever, if only she would forgive him.

She pulled off her bonnet. It hung from the ribbons in her hands as she slowly came to stand before him. "I came to speak to you. We cannot keep going the way we are, Dominic. I cannot bare it."

Her words sparked a flame of hope within him, and he nodded, hoping they could come back to each other.

"I was ashamed, Paris. I have only just admitted my failure to my family, a failure that will impact them and the matches my sisters make. But had I just wanted to marry a woman for her wealth and not care for her in the least, I would have married Lady Esme. Hell, I would have offered to her the moment I left Landon Hall to secure my family's future, but I did not. I cannot marry anyone, wealthy or as poor as I am, for they are not you. I love you. Even when you berate me, reveal my many flaws, it's you I love. I want you as my wife. I want to be a father to your children, to Maya, even if that is a secret we only ever know of. I do not care about the past. I only care for the future, and that cannot be with anyone else but you," he stated, watching, hoping, praying that she would forgive him.

Give him a second chance. Or was it a third by now?

She slipped her hands about his neck and cupped them

around his nape. He swallowed the lump in his throat as longing tore through him.

"You are not the only person who's made errors of judgment. You are not wholly to blame for what happened to me. I should have told you, but we were so young, you were so powerful, and I was nothing compared to your status that I feared being rejected. I thought you would turn your back on me anyway, and then someone else would know my secret. I could not do that to Maya, so I remained silent. I allowed Lord Hervey to think there was more between us than there was, and I married him. And while I did come to care for him, that was wrong. I've always known that, but I blamed you for everything."

"I should never have been so careless to take your innocence and think nothing would come of it," he admitted, hating that he had acted so sinfully. Such a stupid fool.

"What is done is done and I do not want our past, our mistake, or your ruin to change what I think our future can be," she said.

"You want a future with me?" he asked outright, needing to hear her say such wonderous things.

She nodded, stepping between his legs. "I do think that is the case. You love me, and I love you, and I'm wealthy enough to save you this time, and you, me, in return."

Dominic frowned, not sure of her words. "Save you? What do you mean?" he asked.

"Well," she said, slipping onto his lap, her teasing grin making his lips twitch. "I think I'm pregnant and so we had better marry because if it has escaped your notice, I do not have a husband," she teased.

Dominic stilled before he wrenched her into his arms, holding her close. "You're carrying my child?" He shook his head, unable to comprehend the happiness running through him. "I do not know what to say." He laughed, hugging her close.

"You had better ask me to be your wife. We can start there," she said, hugging him.

He pulled back and met her gaze. "Marry me. You're the love of my life, and it would be an honor to be your husband."

"Hmm, let me see," she teased, tapping her chin with her hand. He tickled her, and she squealed before he let her go. "Very well, my lord. I shall marry you. It is only fair, I suppose, since you, too, are the love of my life, and it would be an honor to be your wife."

"So we're betrothed." He rolled her onto the bed, coming down atop her. "Shall we seal the deal with a kiss?"

"I was hoping for a little more than that," she said before he lost himself in a searing kiss that did indeed seal their agreement.

CHAPTER
TWENTY-SIX

Paris stripped what was left of Dominic's attire, not that he was wearing much upon her storming into his room. The lack of a cravat, socks, and shoes enabled her to rip his shirt from his body. Her fingers worked quickly to untie the buttons on his falls.

He, too, was busy with her gown, and they were soon naked on his bed, soon to be her room and home when they married.

The idea warmed a part of her that had long lay dormant and chilled.

She kissed him, reveled in the feel of his hunger, his need for her that was equal to her own.

They came together with a frenzied need. He filled her, thrust into her with such exquisite ability that she gasped. "Dominic," she moaned, pinning her legs behind his back, wanting him deeper, harder than she had before.

"I'm getting a special license. Three days is too long not to have you in my bed," he said, kissing down the side of her neck, electing delicious shivers down her spine.

She moaned, wanting that for herself. Wanting everything that he offered. "You have the most bountiful breasts." His mouth covered one of her nipples, his tongue swirling about her beaded bud, and pleasure shot to her core.

She undulated against him, need and the desire for satisfaction riding her hard. She clutched at him, holding him, undulating and pushing them both toward ecstasy.

It was delightful but not enough, but then she doubted it would ever be enough. Not when it came to Dominic.

Paris flipped Dominic onto his back, straddling him. A sense of power overcame her, and she pressed down on his chest, watching satisfaction and delight twist his features.

He was so handsome, and all hers. The idea that he would soon be her husband was everything she ever wanted in life.

She lifted herself upon him, taking him as he had her. His large manhood filled and inflamed her, and she bore all that he gave and drove toward the pinnacle of pleasure she wanted to reach.

"Dominic," she gasped, the first tremors of her orgasm teasing her.

"You're so beautiful," he said, holding her hips and helping her ride him as she pleased.

The sight of him, his hooded, hungry eyes, and wicked tilt to his lips were too much, and her pleasure rocked through her. Tremor after delicious tremor spasmed within her body. The thought of having Dominic for herself from this day forward, to have him, to love him whenever they wanted, was an addicting elixir that she would never regret.

. . .

Dominic flipped Paris onto the bed. "Roll onto your stomach," he ordered her, not content for their interlude to end with her pleasure.

She did as he bade, and he lifted her hips to kneel before him. He reveled in the sight of her pert ass in the air for a moment. He ran a hand over her soft flesh, reaching around her to cup her cunny, wet and needy, even after attaining ecstasy.

She moaned into the cushions, turning her head to the side. "What are you going to do, Dominic?" she asked him in a hoarse, seductive voice, pressing back on his cock.

He clasped his manhood, rubbing it against her cunny, entering her just slightly, taunting her, teasing her. His balls ached, and his cock hardened to stone.

Hell, he wanted her. He could fuck her all night and day and still not tire from their exertions.

"I'm going to fuck you from behind," he said, slipping into her wet heat.

They groaned in unison, her core tightening, pulling, teasing, and taunting him. The room spun, and he fought not to spend. He was so close. He wanted to come, to take her, mark her as his. Not that she wasn't already.

He knew the incredible gift she had given him this night. Her heart, her soul, and her future. He was the wealthiest man on earth at her acceptance.

She mewled before him as he took her with relentless strokes, pushing, teasing, wanting to make her reach exquisite pleasure again. Watch her come apart in his arms at his behest.

And he could feel she was close. Her cunny tightened about him, wrenching him ever closer to release.

"Yes, Dominic," she gasped, rocking her hips in a circular motion that made the axis of his soul tilt.

"Come for me," he said with each thrust. "Come for me, Paris."

Her hands tightened into the bed sheets, and the first contractions squeezed his cock. It was too much, and he came, spilling his seed into her cunny as she rode her pleasure to completion.

His heart thumped loudly in his ears, his breathing ragged, and he flopped onto the bed, pulling her into his arms and holding her close as they collected themselves.

She sighed, looking up to meet his eyes. "I love you," she admitted, throwing him a smile that reminded him of the first night they had met. When she had been innocent and sweet, and he had wanted her in his bed even then.

"I love you too," he returned, pulling her closer still. "So much. We shall never be parted again." He knew that no matter what occurred in the coming days, weeks, or months, that promise would be true. He could not live without her, and he'd be damned if he cared who knew it.

"My wishes exactly," she said.

He could not have said it better himself.

EPILOGUE

They were married three days later, and within the week, Paris had closed up the Hervey town house and settled her steward at Landon Hall until her son came of age. Of course, they would visit the estate, and she would keep a close eye on the accounts over the next several years, but it was no longer her home.

She was Viscountess Astoridge now, and the thought of such a truth filled her with happiness.

They attended the Duke and Duchess of Derby's ball for their final night in London, having decided to return to Dominic's Surrey estate for the remainder of the Season. There was much to attend, in any case. Dominic's finances for one which needed sorting, and then they could enjoy their little honeymoon, be it at home or elsewhere. It did not matter so long as they were all together.

"You look beautiful this evening, darling," Dominic whispered into her ear as they watched the dancers on the dance floor enjoy a waltz.

She grinned up at him, chuckling. "You have told me multiple times already, husband. I think it is clear to me that you think I do," she teased, unable to wipe the smile from her lips.

"You are ever more beautiful because you carry my child." He slipped his hand to cup her stomach, not that she was showing any signs of being pregnant, but that he knew she was, was enough.

She covered his hand with hers. "Tell me, husband, who is that talking to Lord Billington? I do not recognize him," she asked.

Dominic glanced over toward where he had seen Billington last and smiled. "That is the Duke of Renford. He is a recluse. Well, he had to be after several trysts with married women in London several years ago, before our time, you understand." He paused. "His father had ordered him to return to their estate in Kent, but little is known of him after that. He seemed to heed the warning from his sire before taking on the dukedom only last year."

"He is deadly handsome. Why his hair is as dark as the night sky," she whispered.

Dominic tightened his hold on his wife, not entirely sure he liked the sound of her complimenting other men. "You will make me jealous, madam," he teased.

She chuckled. "Who were the ladies he had affairs with? Do you know?" she asked, glancing about the room, as if she would solve this mystery herself.

"I do not know, but I believe it was written in Whites betting books. I could always look through the past entries and find out."

His wife glanced at him, a wicked light in her eyes, and he knew she wanted him to do that.

"Do you think he's in London to find a wife?"

I doubt it. He's as wicked as they come. He has no family now, no siblings or parents. He may do whatever he pleases, and from what I know of him, he does that most nights."

"Scandalous," she gasped, sipping her ratafia. "Oh look, Ashley is speaking to him."

"The Duchess of Blackhaven, you mean." He was still not used to hearing Paris speak of the Woodville sisters by their given names, not now that all of them were married to wealthy, titled men. But it was the same for all of them. Each used their given names and rarely their titles, such close friends they were. "I believe Blackhaven is an old friend of his and Lord Billington. They would be acquainted through those gentlemen, I would assume." That the duke still owned one of the wickedest gaming hells in London and, from where rumor had it, he had met Ashley Woodville before falling in love with the chit would make sense. Where else would the wicked Duke of Renford make use of his time but around gambling and sex?

"He would be a perfect match for Daphne, do you not think? I shall speak to Ashley about bringing her to town for the Season next year. She is the only one in our social sphere who has not married, and I know that life in Grafton has become a bore. She would enjoy a Season in town."

Dominic sighed, knowing only too well what the Duke of Renford wished for, and it was not a wife. The man was a fool, of course, for there was much to gain from having a woman love you and want you as much as you wanted her.

He studied his wife and saw the contemplation in her eyes. "Do not play matchmaker, Paris. You cannot in any case. You will not be here next year. We'll be in Surrey, remember?"

She smiled but did not stop studying the duke. "Well, before I leave, I shall speak to Ashley. It will not hurt to place Daphne and Renford in close proximity. If they're not in the same room, a match can never come to pass, but one never knows if they are," she said.

Dominic sighed, hoping the poor Daphne did not end her Season next year brokenhearted like all the other ladies who had tried to bring the duke to heel.

"All I ask is that you do not get your hopes up, or the Daphne chit's. That would be unfair to both of you," he cautioned.

His wife waved his words aside. "Do not worry, husband. All will work out well. If I can bring one of England's most sinful viscounts to heel, Daphne can certainly bring to heel a duke. You have not met her. She is marvelous."

He nodded, not doubting that for a moment. "It seems most women from Grafton are," he agreed.

She leaned up and kissed his cheek. "So glad we're in agreement," she said before flouncing toward the Duchess of Blackhaven. He followed, of course. He would follow his wife anywhere, as he promised he would.

Dear Reader,

Thank you for taking the time to read *The Notorious Lord Sin*! I hope you enjoyed the ninth book in my The Wayward Woodvilles series!

I'm so thankful for my readers support. If you're able, I would appreciate an honest review of *The Notorious Lord Sin*. As they say, feed an author, leave a review!

Alternatively, you can keep in contact with me by visiting my website, subscribing to my newsletter or following me online. You can contact me at www.-tamaragill.com.

Tamara Gill

DON'T MISS TAMARA'S OTHER ROMANCE SERIES

The Marquess is Mine

Kiss the Wallflower

A Midsummer Kiss

A Kiss at Mistletoe

A Kiss in Spring

To Fall For a Kiss

A Duke's Wild Kiss

To Kiss a Highland Rose

Lords of London

To Bedevil a Duke

To Madden a Marquess

To Tempt an Earl

To Vex a Viscount

To Dare a Duchess

To Marry a Marchioness

To Marry a Rogue

Only an Earl Will Do

Only a Duke Will Do

Only a Viscount Will Do

Only a Marquess Will Do

Only a Lady Will Do

A Time Traveler's Highland Love

To Conquer a Scot

To Save a Savage Scot

To Win a Highland Scot

A Stolen Season

A Stolen Season

A Stolen Season: Bath

A Stolen Season: London

Scandalous London

A Gentleman's Promise

A Captain's Order

A Marriage Made in Mayfair

High Seas & High Stakes

His Lady Smuggler

Her Gentleman Pirate

A Wallflower's Christmas Wreath

Daughters Of The Gods

Banished

Guardian

Fallen

Stand Alone Books

Defiant Surrender

A Brazen Agreement

To Sin with Scandal

Outlaws

ABOUT THE AUTHOR

Tamara is an Australian author who grew up in an old mining town in country South Australia, where her love of history was founded. So much so, she made her darling husband travel to the UK for their honeymoon, where she dragged him from one historical monument and castle to another.

A mother of three, her two little gentlemen in the making, a future lady (she hopes) keep her busy in the real world, but whenever she gets a moment's peace she loves to write romance novels in an array of genres, including regency, medieval and time travel.

Made in the USA
Columbia, SC
26 December 2022